The problem Russell had keeping the shirt on his back...

The hulking brute stomped through the restaurant toward Russell's table. The maître d' waved frantically to one of the waiters. "Stop him," he mouthed. The waiter gave him an are-you-crazy look.

Someone screamed. A waiter dropped a dish. A headline flashed through Russell's mind. English Professor Strangled At Chez Nous. His Last Words: "Please Pass The Sautéed Spinach."

The incredible hulk reached the table filled with Russell's future in-laws and placed both hands on Russell's shoulders. "The time has come for this dude to face the music."

"I'll always love you," Russell's fiancée said, easing her hand from his.

In a rush of movement the hulk grabbed the lapels of Russell's shirt and yanked.

Cool air assaulted Russell's bare chest. He closed his eyes, not wanting to witness anything else. Ever. In this lifetime. Or the next.

For a long moment there was a deafening silence. Not even the faintest chink of glass or whispered comment could be heard in the room.

Until his fiancée spoke. "Who is *Liz?*"

Dear Reader,

Trying to choose one romantic comedy movie as a favorite is an almost impossible task! I don't know if I could narrow down my many, many choices, but that is the question we've been asking our writers as part of our Let's Celebrate sweepstakes. Take a moment to read what our authors have chosen and fill out the entry form to win a collection of romantic comedy videos.

Judy Griffith Gill returns to LOVE & LAUGHTER with *Lady on Top*. Judy made a lot of fans with *There's Something About The Nanny* (LOVE & LAUGHTER #7). *Romantic Times* said, "Judy Griffith Gill's magical storytelling will charm and enthrall readers." Judy continues to delight with her new book, the story of the quiet, prim and proper librarian who decides it's time to add spice to her life!

Colleen Collins has had an interesting and varied career, everything from public relations to working as a personal assistant in Hollywood. Her love for the movies is apparent in her story *Right Chest, Wrong Name*. Have fun, and as you read this dizzying, madcap adventure you will find it really harks back to the great screwball comedies. You can even play talent agent and cast your own movie in your mind!

What's your favorite romantic comedy movie?

With love and laughter,

Malle Vallik

Malle Vallik
Associate Senior Editor

RIGHT CHEST, WRONG NAME
Colleen Collins

Harlequin Books

TORONTO • NEW YORK • LONDON
AMSTERDAM • PARIS • SYDNEY • HAMBURG
STOCKHOLM • ATHENS • TOKYO • MILAN
MADRID • WARSAW • BUDAPEST • AUCKLAND

ISBN 0-373-44026-X

RIGHT CHEST, WRONG NAME

Copyright © 1997 by Colleen Collins

This edition published by arrangement with Harlequin Books S.A.

® and TM are trademarks of the publisher. Trademarks indicated with ® are registered in the United States Patent and Trademark Office, the Canadian Trade Marks Office and in other countries.

Printed in U.S.A.

A funny thing happened...

As a kid, I remember my dad hiding scary books from me, claiming I shouldn't read them because I had an "overactive" imagination. Of course, I'd find the books and read them anyway. And then I'd imagine stories even more elaborate and wild than what I had read! I *still* have an overactive imagination...but now I funnel my dreams and fantasies into writing my favorite type of story: romance.

—Colleen Collins

To my father, Dale Collins,
who always believed in my dreams.

1

"DARLING, YOU SOUND like a broken cappuccino machine," murmured Charlotte, her voice oozing disapproval.

Russell juggled the receiver while attempting to sit up in bed, but couldn't. If he *sounded* like a wreck over the phone, he could only imagine what he looked like. He pressed his head back down into his pillow. Wishing his damn headache would stop pounding, he tried to remember just what he'd done the night before.... He remembered Drake's picking him up...he remembered their driving to Satiricon, a restaurant-bar frequented by actors, poets and other Los Angeles wanna-bes...

After that, his mind went as blank as an amnesiac's.

"What mischief did you and your friends get into at your bachelor party last night?" she continued.

She always had a way of saying "your friends" as though they were a pack of degenerate water buffalo. Professors deserved to be several notches higher up on the food chain, he thought. Which he would have said if his tongue wasn't swollen to twice its size.

"You didn't do anything...bad...did you, Russell?"

"Bad?" He tried to laugh, but it came out like a bark.

"Bad. As in *naughty*."

He heard her piqued tone but knew she'd never admit to such a base emotion as jealousy. Charlotte Maday, the woman he was to wed in a week, came from a family who bled blue. Exhibiting raw emotion was akin to burping in public.

"Char, the only *bad* thing I've ever done is wear mismatched socks. When I die, my greatest sin will be sartorial disharmony.''

She laughed softly. ''Well, you know what they say about those parties. It's the groom's last fling with bachelorhood and anything goes. But don't worry, darling, I forgive whatever you did.''

Pain ripped through his skull, and Russell winced. Even if he had been bad, he didn't remember a blasted thing. *That* would be the height of irony. Russell Harrington finally rips loose, for the first time in his thirty-five years, and he can't recall one single decadent moment.

''Too many Wild Turkeys,'' he croaked, ''is all you need forgive, my love.''

''Wild Turkeys? The drinks or your friends?''

She knew his drink of choice was Wild Turkey on the rocks. He didn't know whether to be impressed or insulted at her play on words. Mostly he was surprised. Usually Charlotte had the wit of a bank vault.

''The pool party starts at noon,'' she said, shifting into an all-business tone. ''Be punctual. I want you there to greet Mommy's family when they arrive—after all, they flew all the way from London to meet my husband-to-be. And Russell...''

''Yes?''

''Please wear matching socks.''

After ending the conversation, he untangled himself from the bedsheets and stumbled to the bathroom—all the while counting up just how many Wild Turkeys he'd downed last night. Had it been four? Five? Six?

He had always been a two-drink man. ''What happened to moderation in everything?'' he asked himself, cursing his friends for not complying with his bachelor-party request. Drake, his friend since childhood, fellow professor and unrepentant wild man had hooted when Russell had laid the ground rules for his bachelor party: no strippers, no mud wrestling—no activity that might besmirch Charlotte's family name. After all, the Madays were society people. Scandal was a greater fear than death or disease.

He shuddered when his feet hit the bathroom's cold tile floor. If only he could turn around and go back to bed.

"Pool party," he reminded himself. He'd put on his best front and accommodate Char's request. Make the family rounds, exchange a few pleasantries, play the role she liked best: the erudite, cultured English literature professor. After fulfilling his duties, he'd slink into some lawn chair, preferably one in the shade, and nurse his hangover for the rest of the afternoon.

He tossed back a few aspirin and splashed cold water on his face. Grappling for a towel, he squinted into the mirror.

Then he jerked upright and stared at his reflection, blinking back drops of water. "Good Lord. They stuck me in a wind tunnel."

His hair, usually neatly parted and combed, sprang from his head as though he'd been struck by lightning. "Can too many Wild Turkeys do that?" he asked himself as he stared with horror at his reflection.

Something caught his eye in the mirror. Russell's gaze dropped.

"What in the h—"

Over his pectoral muscle was a small patch of white. A bandage. Gingerly, he pulled it off.

Underneath, on his skin, was not a wound but a small, neat drawing.

"A red heart?" His voice cracked on the word "heart." Something—a word?—was scrawled across it, which in the mirror looked like gibberish. He looked down at his chest and tried to read it upside down.

"Liz?" he said, frowning. He looked at his reflection again as though it were someone else who might explain all this to him.

Then, slowly, he grinned. "I see. A joke." He gave his head a knowing shake, then instantly regretted it as his brain began throbbing mercilessly yet again from the back-and-forth motion. He grabbed the towel and patted his face dry, guessing what happened the night before. "The boys stuck some decal on me, knowing I'd wake up and think

I'd gotten a tattoo.'' He imagined their glee, anticipating the mild coronary he'd have after finding some strange woman's name stenciled on his chest.

"Very funny, guys," Russell muttered sarcastically.

He tossed the towel onto the rack behind him, then touched the edge of the heart to pull the thing off. He grimaced. His skin was extraordinarily tender.

He lightly traced his finger around the heart's edge. No plastic ridge. Just…skin.

A cold foreboding inched down his spine.

This was no decal. This was…

"Good Lord," he croaked. "I got a tattoo. A heart tattoo with the name 'Liz' on it."

Muttering a string of expletives, he stomped to the phone and punched in Drake's number.

"What did you guys do to me? And who the hell is Liz?" demanded Russell.

"Russell?" There was a rumpling sound on the other end. "That you?" Drake said sleepily.

"Yes, it's me," he answered between his teeth. "And I want to know what Liz is doing on my chest."

"Hey, buddy, your personal life is your business." Drake lowered his voice. "You're making a phone call at a time like this? Is she still on your chest?"

"Drake, that's not what I'm talking about." Russell blew out a gust of air. "I didn't want strippers or mud wrestling, so my friends decided the next best thing was to stain my skin with another woman's name?"

"Stain?" Pause. "You…you got a *tattoo?*" Drake emitted a low whistle. "We wondered what happened after you left the restaurant."

"After I left?"

"With…that biker babe."

Russell blinked and stared at the Toulouse-Lautrec print, *La Toilette*, on his far wall. His gaze roamed up the woman's uncovered legs, over her bare back, to her red hair caught in a chignon at the nape of her neck. "Biker babe?"

he repeated slowly. "You mean, I left with some strange woman?"

Drake chuckled. "Don't know about strange, but she was hot stuff, I can tell you that. Last seen, you were on the back of her Harley, the two of you driving off into the night like the last shot of some Hollywood movie." Silence. "Buddy, I can't believe *you* got a tattoo. Next you'll tell me William Buckley's gonna pose nude for *Playgirl*."

Fighting down a surge of panic, Russell craned his neck to check the clock on his nightstand. "I'm due at Charlotte's in two hours. I can't show up branded like this. I must find who did it—and make them take it off." An annoying thought crossed his mind—did he pay for this atrocity as well? "And they better not charge me, either," he added with self-righteous anger. On a university professor's salary, and with an upcoming wedding and honeymoon, every penny counted.

"Hey, if they make you pay, don't argue the issue. Hand over some plastic—I'll reimburse you. After all, it wouldn't have happened if I'd made you stay put."

"You don't have the money. Even if you did, I wouldn't take it." Drake blew his paychecks on wine, women and jazz. And not necessarily in that order.

"Count it as part of my wedding gift. Besides, it's no skin off my...uh, never mind."

Skin. Russell glanced down at his tattoo. Was it his imagination or did the heart look bigger from this angle? The word "Liz" seemed larger, too. "How am I going to ask them to remove it when I don't even know where I was last night?" A sinking sensation rocked his insides, reminding him of a roller-coaster ride he had taken as a kid.

"This is insane," he continued. "I wake up with a mysterious tattoo. Don't know whose name is on it, or why I got it. And now I'm going to try and find out where it happened so I can get the damn thing off in time for Charlotte's pool party. While I'm performing these heroic tasks, maybe I can also bring about world peace."

"Pool party?" asked Drake. "As in swim trunks, bare chests?"

Russell squeezed his eyes shut. After a moment, he said calmly, "I have no choice. I have to confess this to Charlotte."

"You'll end up with another tattoo. This one shaped like a certain lady's fist. But this time, no name. Just the imprint of Charlotte's megawatt engagement ring."

The ring that had cost Russell two months' salary. He opened his eyes and stared again at *La Toilette*, remembering the story about the man who willed himself into a painting and escaped his miserable life. How convenient that would be right now...

"Something was written across the side of that babe's Harley," offered Drake. "I remember now—a Tennessee Williams play...*The*...*The Rose Tattoo*? Bingo! The Rose Tattoo. That must be the scene of the crime."

"Wonderful. I was abducted by a cult of flower-loving tattoo artists."

"Or a cult of theater-loving tattoo artists."

"Drake, spare me. Maybe someday I'll laugh at all this...but definitely not now." Russell grabbed the phone book from underneath the nightstand and began flipping through the yellow pages. "Tanning Salons. Tarpaulins. Tattoos...here we go. Good Lord. There are more tattoo parlors than churches listed in this thing."

"That's L.A. for you—a city that knows its priorities."

Russell's finger slid down a list of names. "Found it! The Rose Tattoo. Hollywood Boulevard. Open every day of the week, including Sunday."

"For the post-church crowd, no doubt."

"I'm getting dressed and going there."

"Russ," Drake said, his tone turning serious. "I'm sorry, buddy. Jeez...you don't think you'll need a skin graft, do you?"

Russell's stomach did a triple gainer. "Spare me the graphics. And do me a favor."

"Anything."

"Call Charlotte. Tell her...I have an...emergency meeting with a student. Tell her the guy went ballistic and...demanded a meeting to discuss a low grade I gave him. And that I might be a little late to her pool party."

"Sure thing. Pissed-off student. Big F."

Russell was already stepping out of his boxers. "Something like that. Don't overdo it, okay?" He taught literature at UCLA. Drake taught drama at Santa Monica Community College. Or high drama, Russell sometimes accused him of. All their lives, Drake had always been the one who got into the colorful larger-than-life situations. How Russell managed to land smack in the middle of this one had to mean the Fates were spinning out of control.

"Don't worry," assured Drake. "I'll handle it." A moment's pause. "Pool party?" He made a thoughtful sound. "As a backup plan, think one-piece suit."

THIRTY MINUTES LATER, Russell was on Hollywood Boulevard. He had walked slowly down this stretch of storefront window displays filled with tacky lingerie, videos and leather ensembles that exposed key parts of the anatomy, searching for The Rose Tattoo. The stench of exhaust, grease—and some smells he feared to identify—had only intensified his hangover, making his head feel like a demolition crew was attacking his brain with drills.

"Hey, brother, wanna buy a T-shirt?" A bearded man in a rainbow-colored beret and a T-shirt that said Exercise Your Rights, Not Your Body materialized from a store's doorway. He raised his chubby arm, draped with a pile of shirts.

"No thanks," mumbled Russell, squinting at the next storefront, which featured a mannequin on all fours, a rocket strapped to her back. The sign in the window read Hot Fourth of July Sale! Russell swallowed, hard, and tried not to stare at the lacy red number that barely covered the mannequin's essentials.

"Five bucks." The guy waved open a T-shirt that read Jack Nicholson For President.

"No. Thank you." Russell kept walking, hoping his averted gaze would dissuade the freelance clothing merchant.

It didn't. The guy scurried alongside. "Buy two, and I'll throw in a steak knife."

Russell stopped and did a double take. "Steak knife?"

The man shrugged and scratched his scraggly beard. "Hey, some of my best customers almost have a set."

Russell glanced at his watch. Ten-forty. He'd need to be heading to Charlotte's soon. "Say, know where I can find The Rose Tattoo?"

"Best ink in Hollywood, brother." The man grinned and flexed his free arm, displaying a peace symbol with the words Mum And Dad written around it. "I like the traditional look. But you?" He rolled his eyes to someplace above Russell's eyebrows. "Definitely something wild." He pointed to a window several doors down.

Russell was heading in the direction the man had indicated when a roaring sound distracted him. A gleaming white motorcycle cruised down the street, pulled an illegal U and lurched to a stop at the curb only a few feet away. The diminutive rider—encased in a sleeveless, fringed white-leather ensemble—cut the engine and slid off the bike in one sensuous motion.

She pulled off her goggles and shook her head. Her blazing red hair cascaded like fire to her waist, sparking gold and copper in the bright L.A. sunshine.

"The loose train of thy amber-dropping hair," Russell thought, recalling a line from Milton. A ripple of indistinct memory flowed over him, accompanied by a feeling of…happiness.

He sucked in a breath of warm air. Ridiculous. He didn't know this woman. Or *any* women of her ilk.

Yet Drake claimed that he, Russell, had ridden off on the back of a Harley. He glanced at the bike. Along the back fender were the words Harley Davidson, the letters entwined with red and pink roses.

Along the gas tank were the words The Rose Tattoo.

"Russell," she said. "Back for more?" Her lips, as red as the roses stenciled on her bike, spread into a wide, luscious grin.

She had a smoky Lauren Bacall voice. The kind that turned Humphrey Bogart types into putty. A second memory heated his insides. His hands gripping a small waist, feeling the soft, buttery texture of her leather outfit. Cool blasts of summer air hitting his face as they flew past a blur of neon lights...

He would have responded, but all his body functions had gone on strike. He cleared his throat. Miraculously, his lips moved, followed by a raspy sound that used to be his voice. "More what?" he croaked.

She jutted out her hip and placed one fist against it. "More tattoos." Her eyes narrowed slightly. "What did you think I meant, Russell?"

He coughed and quickly looked up and down the street, half expecting someone to say "Cut" and whisk him out of this *Twilight Zone* episode. "Same thing. More tattoos," he mumbled. "Not that I want more," he added quickly. "In fact, I want this—" he gestured with primitive motions toward his chest "—off. Want off. Now."

Every day he stood in front of hundreds of students, giving lectures on Faulkner, Yeats, Lawrence—yet here he was standing in front of this...biker babe...acting like some recently thawed Neanderthal.

She took another step forward. Her perfume reached him. Spicy, exotic. Definitely unlike the delicate flowery scent Charlotte wore.

"It's not bothering you, is it?" she asked huskily. She pulled off one of her white leather gloves, exposing a small hand with bloodred nails, their tips embellished with tiny white flowers. "I took extra care with that tat so it would heal quickly."

"Tat?"

"Tattoo."

"Right. Tattoo." Good Lord, what had happened to him last night? This was the kind of woman who appeared in your wildest dreams but never invaded your reality. "I want it off," he repeated, congratulating himself on completing a sentence. He swiped at a bead of sweat that had broken loose from his hairline. Had the temperature risen in the past few minutes?

She followed the movement of his hand, her green eyes sparking with humor. "Uh, what happened to your hair?"

He raised his hand and felt the spiky mess that topped his head. No wonder that T-shirt vendor had rolled his eyes skyward, saying he should get a "wild" tattoo—something to match the chaos on Russell's head, no doubt. In his rush to get dressed and out the door, he'd forgotten to comb his hair.

She gave her head a small shake, which made her long red curls shimmer in the sunlight. "And as to removing your tattoo, I can't."

Can't? Visions of his honeymoon night loomed in his mind like an ominous tidal wave. Charlotte seeing the tattoo. Seeing the name "Liz."

Tears.

Recriminations.

Annulment.

Was a man expected to pay alimony if the marriage ended after one night, he wondered bleakly.

He began pacing the sidewalk. "I would never have gotten this ludicrous tattoo if I had been sober. You took advantage of my inebriated state."

"I took advanta…?"

He stopped and stared accusingly at her. "Is that what lonely tattoo artists do on Friday nights? Roam restaurants looking for some innocent man to cut loose from the pack and then brand him for life?"

"Me, lonely?" She rose to her full height—which he guessed to be a little over five feet—and gave him a penetrating stare. He presumed she was trying to be formidable, but in actuality, she looked damn sexy. He instantly regretted his words. This woman had probably never known a lonely night in her life. What man wouldn't desire a woman with the allure of Venus and the body of a sex kitten?

He shifted his stance, wishing his brain would react instead of his body.

"Look, if I want a date, all I have to do is answer my phone." Her eyes shot fire.

His stomach flinched as though he'd been socked. "I— I spoke too hastily," he mumbled.

"And I don't need to cut some—" she looked him up and down "—'innocent' guy loose from the pack."

"No, no you don't," offered Russell. Although cutting his tongue out was a good idea. He made a mental note to remove it after he removed the tattoo. It was the least he could do to make amends.

"And," she continued, her gaze narrowing.

"There's more?"

She arched one eyebrow. "I don't need to 'brand' a man. What do I look like—a cowboy?"

Hardly.

"I especially don't need to brand some snooty English professor who picked *me* up." With a swishing sound, she walked past him to a door marked The Rose Tattoo and shoved a key into the lock.

He turned, slowly. "*I* picked *you* up?" A small surge of pride welled within him. If he had charmed this exotic-Venus-sex-kitten, maybe he should have started overimbibing years ago.

She twisted the knob and gave the bottom of the door a brusque kick with her lizard-skin boot. "Impressed with yourself?" She gave the door a shove and it opened with a popping sound.

He couldn't deny that he was. He never made the first move except in chess. Charlotte had made the overtures in their relationship. Planned their dates. Arranged the wedding. He had liked the practical ease their union promised. Anything impetuous or fanciful made him anxious. His life had always been one sensible, logical decision after another. No chasing after silly dreams.

Until last night.

The memories again struggled to resurface. He vaguely recalled nuzzling long, silky hair and inhaling its flowery scent. Recalled brushing his lips against petal-soft cheeks...

Sensations swirled in his brain. Heat flared in his groin.

"If I did pick you up," he said thickly, his mind racing with the sensual memories, "I'm impressed I had the nerve to approach a woman as good-looking as you."

She turned her head slightly and cast him a long look. A rose hue crept up her neck. She parted her lips as though to speak but said nothing.

He felt as though he'd pulled back a curtain and seen what lay beneath her tough exterior. Inside, she was vulnerable. Soft. The antithesis of her tough biker-babe act.

He studied her, drawn to something he couldn't put a finger on. Suddenly, a thought crashed through his mind. "Is your name Liz?"

She waited a beat before answering. "Millicent."

He frowned. The name didn't ring a bell. But at least "Millicent" hadn't been engraved across his chest...not that it explained why "Liz" was there, but he'd deal with that later.

Later. He didn't have time to deal with anything "later." He had problems to deal with *now*.

He glanced at his watch. Quarter to eleven. Panic flooded his veins. He had to leave in thirty minutes. How would he hide the tattoo? He could cover it with a bandage, but what kind of wound needed a four-inch-square covering? He'd have to concoct one story about what kind of wound, another for how he got it. Stories, deceit, flesh wounds. Bad hair. His head throbbed with the prospect of facing Charlotte and her family. "If only I hadn't been drunk last night," he muttered.

"Let's get something straight." She leaned one hand against the doorjamb and stared him down. "I have never given a tat to anyone I thought was pickled. If you had downed one too many, then you're the only drunk I've met who can talk about the symbolism of Yeats without slurring once."

He was momentarily taken back. "I sound like a fun drunk," he murmured, regaining his senses. "Good thing I don't teach calculus."

Her gaze traveled over his face, the look in her eyes softening. "Russell, life's too short to be—" She stopped herself and gave her head a small shake. "Never mind." She tapped one colorful fingernail against the opened door. "Maybe I can do *something*."

Something? Thoughts tumbled in his head. Sear it off with a hot fire poker? Cut the tattoo out of his flesh with a steak knife? Painless alternatives compared with what Charlotte might do.

"Come on in, Russell."

The smoky quality of her voice trailed through the air and wound around his mind, fogging his thoughts. He felt intoxicated by her presence.

"You coming?" she asked. "It's cool."

It took him a moment to realize it was a slang term, not air-conditioning. He should leave. Walk away. He had a sane life on the other side of this Hollywood looking glass. A respectable career, a lovely fiancée from a prestigious family, a future with two-point-five kids.

Yet even as these thoughts poured through his brain, a single truth bubbled to the forefront—he had never experienced the emotions that he was feeling now. Hot, alive. As though he were skirting the edge of some gut-level need that had eluded him his entire life.

He moved toward the opened door. *This is only about getting my tattoo removed,* he rationalized, shoving down his more primal urges. *After all, that's why I'm here. To erase last night's foolish act.*

He almost believed himself.

Inside, it was soothingly dark, illuminated only by the sunlight that streamed in through the open door. As his eyes adjusted to the dimness, he saw a large overstuffed couch against the left wall. In the center of the room, a wing chair.

Next to it, on a small oval table, a stained-glass lamp that glinted bright blues, reds and greens as rays of light pierced its globe.

Hardly the type of room he expected to find in a tattoo parlor. No two ways about it—the room had a homey quality. The biker babe was an earth mother at heart?

She leaned over to pick up mail lying on the floor. Sunlight traced her bottom, illuminating its firm roundness. *There should be a law about bodies like hers wearing clinging white leather,* he decided.

"Contemplating Yeats again?"

He raised his gaze in time to meet hers.

"Just his symbolism," he quipped, relieved when her lips curled into a slow smile.

She pulled off her other glove and tossed both, along with the mail, onto the top of a bookcase. Then she nodded toward the wing chair.

"Take a load off your mind, Professor, and let's check that tat."

After he sat down, she stood in front of him and crossed her arms under her chest. The sun backlit her, the yellow haze outlining her taut contours. He stared at her small waist and how it flared subtly into slightly rounded hips.

"Take off your shirt," she whispered.

2

"SHIRT?" HE REPEATED, swallowing.

"You know, the thing you're wearing that buttons down the front."

"Yes, of course." He eased out a slow breath and began fumbling with the buttons.

"Here, let me help," she offered, kneeling in front of him.

She expertly undid the buttons. Cool air swept over his skin as she pulled the shirt off and tossed it onto the back of the chair.

Then she leaned closer. He imagined he saw the pulse throbbing at the base of her throat. His senses felt drenched with her scent. Gently probing the skin around the tattoo, she whispered, "How does that feel?"

Better than he wanted to admit. "Little sore—not bad, though."

"Good."

That voice again. Like honey and whisky. Her touch like fire on his skin. He closed his eyes and tried to recall the prologue to *The Canterbury Tales*. Letters jumped and danced in his mind like drops of water on a skillet.

"You *wanted* that tattoo, Russell," she said quietly.

Her voice betrayed her hurt. He opened his eyes and stared into her face. He'd hurt her? By asking for the tattoo to be removed?

"I tried to talk you out of getting the tat, but you *insisted*," she continued, her hands stroking the edge of the tattoo. "Why, Russell?"

She leaned back and watched him in the pool of sunlight.

Last night he had been a motormouth, babbling on and on about books, poets and life. He'd confessed his dreams. Demanded she share her own. His endless stream of words hadn't stopped even when they'd kissed...

She wetted her lips, savoring the memory. Either the guy really didn't remember last night, or he wanted a quick exit from memory lane. She knew the type. Love-'em-and-leave-'em guys with egos the size of the Hollywood sign.

Yet Russell Harrington had seemed different. A sensitive kind of guy. Caring. Vulnerable, even. She couldn't dismiss last night without knowing the truth. Were her memories that far off base?

"Why?" she asked again, studying his perplexed stare.

His eyebrows pressed together. "Why did *I* want the tattoo?"

She nodded.

"I have no idea why you tattooed me..." His voice trailed off.

She turned away from him and began switching on lights. An ache filled her as she remembered his lips taking hers. Maybe he was sensitive, but his kiss had been firm, authoritative.

So unlike the man who now seemed baffled by the entire experience. She clicked on another light, keeping her face carefully turned away so he wouldn't see her disappointment.

"Elizabeth Barrett Browning," he announced suddenly.

She stiffened, then looked over her shoulder and caught him staring at the framed quotation hanging on the wall.

"'Yet half a beast is the great god Pan/To Laugh, as he sits by the river,/Making a poet out of a man,'" he read aloud. "I seem to recall reading that last night..." His voice trailed off again.

"You did. With gusto." She played with one of the beaded fringes on her jacket, avoiding his eyes.

"Elizabeth Barrett Browning," he repeated slowly. "Elizabeth..."

She looked up and saw him pondering his tattoo.

His head jerked up. "You tattooed me with her name. Well, no, a nineties rendition of her name. Liz."

"There wasn't time to write the entire name—"

"Thank God!" He raked a hand through his hair. "Elizabeth Barrett Browning... Doesn't her name alone cover most of the alphabet?" He leaned back his head and stared at the ceiling. "But why stop there? You could have stenciled most of the *Sonnets from the Portuguese* on me by dawn." He gestured wildly to the ceiling. "Across my chest, around my back, down my buttocks..."

He lurched forward and leveled her a wild-eyed look. "Because I'm an English professor, you probably thought I'd like that. A poet's name engraved on me for the rest of my life." Suddenly, his shoulders slumped and he dropped his head into his hands. "The rest of my life. Wonderful. Not only do I teach literature, now I wear it as well."

"Sorry," she whispered. She'd had a few irate customers in her day, but never someone who acted as though his life was at an end because of one simple tattoo.

He sighed audibly. "Worse, no one will ever know it's a poet. Liz. People will think I have a movie-star fetish."

"We compromised on Liz because—"

"Please," he interrupted, holding up a hand. "I can figure out why. Fewer letters. Vanna White would be proud."

Despite her better instincts, she felt sorry for the guy.

"It's healing well," she said softly. "But your skin's too sensitive to try removing it. Come back in two weeks." By then she'd have forgotten last night. Or at least have put it behind her.

"Two weeks?" He leaped to his feet, then raised a hand to his head as though the movement jolted something loose. "I can't get married," he finally said, speaking slowly, "wearing this scarlet letter. Letters. My future wife will murder me in cold blood—and undoubtedly get off on grounds of temporary tattoo insanity."

"So you're going through with it, Max?"

He frowned and lowered his hand. "How'd you know about Max? I discussed my screenplay? With you?"

"I don't look like the kind of girl to discourse intellec-
tually?"

"One doesn't discourse. It's a noun."

"Well, this *one* does. I discourse regularly." She twisted
a strand of hair around her finger, wondering how much to
divulge about the night before.

"We shared our dreams," she began hesitantly. "You
told me about your screenplay, and how you wanted to
write under the name Max, not Russell. Called Max your
alter ego, the wild, rugged writer you secretly are." She
started to smile at the memory but stopped. He had been
under the Wild Turkey influence. Anything they had
"shared" was now hers alone to recall.

Disappointment tugged at her heart.

"Enough chat," she said briskly, not wanting to dwell
on why she felt let down. "Come back in a few days—I'll
see what I can do. Keeping your chest covered until then
shouldn't be a problem."

"So it can be taken off, you think, in a few days?"

"Maybe we can do a cover-up. Enlarge the heart.
Change 'Liz' to 'Charlotte.'"

He blinked. "I discussed her last night, too?"

"Among other things..." Her chest constricted. She
made a silent promise not to be gullible the next time an
intelligent, kind, decent guy came along. Especially one
with a fondness for Wild Turkey and Yeats.

"We seem to have discussed a lot of things last night."

"Yes." Her voice was barely above a whisper.

"Last night," he continued, taking a step toward her.
"We...we didn't, did we?"

She tried to look indifferent, but a tell-tale hot rush
flooded her face.

"Did we?" he persisted, moving closer.

Her eyes locked with his. She knew she should detour
this conversation and deny last night had been more than
two people shooting the breeze. She opened her mouth to

make some glib comment, but the liquid look in his eyes stopped her. The look that had made her melt last night.

Her knees began to shake.

She made a small, confused motion with her hand, but speech failed her. Memories from last night heated her insides. She nervously pulled a strand of hair around her face, hoping it might hide the hot flush that burned her cheeks. Playing the shy schoolgirl had never been her style. But something about being near this man unnerved her. She—who loved to crank her Harley full blast for the speed and the rush of adrenaline—felt dangerously out of control next to this decent, flustered English professor.

He rubbed his thumb along his jaw. "I think you're answering my question," he said quietly.

"We...we almost did," she finally said, the intensity evident in her lowered voice.

The seconds stretched into a full minute.

She closed her eyes, chiding herself for spilling the truth. It would have been better if she'd just lied. Said nothing happened. Zilch. After all, this guy was headed to the altar in a week. And her life...well, it had its own complications and she had her plans. "I wish last night had never happened," she admitted under her breath.

She felt his nearness even before she opened her eyes. Like a wave of heat, it enveloped her.

"Don't say that," he whispered, his warm breath stroking her cheek.

He was too close. She should pull away.

She drew a breath, inhaling traces of his woodsy cologne. The familiar scent discharged a small thrill that zigzagged down her spine.

She opened her eyes. "Russell," she murmured, but it came out more like a plea.

She sighed when his lips brushed lightly against her own. Her hands trembled. Her lips parted in expectation—hoping, desiring his mouth to possess hers again as it had last night...

"What the hell's goin' on here?" thundered a deep voice.

They both reeled back. A mountain with a head on top blocked the opened doorway.

"Liz," growled the mountain, his voice rumbling through the room like an oncoming storm, "who you lip-lockin' with?"

"Liz?" repeated Russell, jerking his gaze to her. "What happened to Millicent?"

She shrugged. "Everybody calls me Liz...sometimes Elizabeth...because of..." She motioned to the quotation on the wall behind her as though that explained everything. Then she turned back to the mountain and sighed audibly. "Raven, this is none of your business."

Mt. Raven snorted and stomped into the room. The stained-glass lamp rattled.

After halting in front of Russell, Raven unzipped his black leather jacket.

Russell's blood chilled. *He's going to pull a gun on me.* Tomorrow's headlines flashed through his mind: *English Professor Shot In Cold Blood. Last Words: "Don't Tell Charlotte About The Tat."*

Raven shrugged out of his jacket and dropped it onto the floor, never breaking eye contact with Russell. A black T-shirt, with rips instead of armholes, stretched across Raven's refrigerator-size chest. Stenciled on the shirt in white block letters were the words Don't Mess With This Mutha.

Russell revised the headline. *English Professor Shot In Cold Blood By One Bad Mutha.*

Raven's top lip curled, giving his Fu Manchu mustache a sinister arch. He growled and flexed an oversize biceps tattooed with a garish red, yellow and blue iguana. The reptile slithered as the muscle rippled and bulged. Until that very moment, Russell had never fully appreciated the power of nonverbal communication.

To avoid Raven's death-defying gaze, Russell concentrated on the skull-and-crossbones earring dangling from his pierced earlobe. A motion distracted him. He looked down at Raven's hands, which he clenched and opened rhythmically.

Hands the size of chickens.

Hairy chickens.

Hands that could easily compress a human-size skull into an earring.

"Raven, cut the testosterone theatrics," interrupted Liz.

Russell slid his gaze to her. She stood across the room, her hands on her hips. Sunlight streamed through the open door and swirled about her red hair in a fiery halo. At that moment, she look like Venus on fire.

"If you must know what we were doing," she continued, enunciating each word as though Raven suddenly didn't understand English, "we were discussing his tat."

Raven's leather pants crinkled as he leaned closer to Russell, who suppressed the urge to cough at the whiff of cigarette breath.

"Where is it?" demanded Raven, narrowing his eyes. "On his lip?" His gaze lowered. His Fu Manchu mustache drooped. "What the hell," he said slowly, "is *my* fiancée's name—" he stabbed his index finger into Russell's shoulder and loomed closer "—doin' on *your* chest?"

Russell closed his eyes, wondering when his life would start flashing by. But the way his luck was going today, he'd probably get somebody else's life. His last few seconds on Earth would be spent reliving things he'd never done, seeing people he'd never known...

He breathed in, the act reassuring him he was still alive. Swallowing back the small boulder in his throat, he slowly opened his eyes.

"Small world, isn't it?" he said, willing himself to sound conversational. "Elizabeth—Liz—is the same name as...my grandmother's. Grandmother Liz, we called her." He attempted to smile, but his upper lip stuck to his teeth. He hoped Raven wouldn't misinterpret the contorted lip as some kind of barbaric facial challenge.

"Grandmother, my a—" Raven roared like a wounded

King Kong and raised his meaty hands in the air, the fingers curled around an imaginary neck.

Not imaginary for long, Russell thought, instinctively springing back in a *salto in dietro,* a maneuver he used in his college fencing days.

Raven's brow compressed into a perplexed frown. "What the...?"

Taking advantage of Raven's momentary confusion, Russell jumped aggressively forward in a short *flèche.*

Raven shook his head, which made his braid flick back and forth like a dog's tail. Russell swore Raven's ears flattened as he raised his hands higher. Then, with a primitive war cry, he smashed them down.

Russell lunged to the right, barely missing the intended blow.

Unable to stop his momentum, Raven careened forward, his massive bulk propelling him across the room, where he crashed into the wall, headfirst. The loud thud was followed by a small, confused grunt.

Liz expelled a weighty sigh. "I just fixed a hole in that wall." She looked at Russell and crossed her arms. "Are you two through with your macho demo?"

"Macho...?" He swiped at a drop of sweat that inched down his jaw. "I believe Crow started it."

"Raven."

"Yes, of course." He glanced at the black heap against the back wall. "Raven." Russell stared at his shirt, which lay strewn across the chair that Raven's bulk had shoved clear across the room. The same chair that Raven now gripped for support as he tried to heave his frame up into a standing position.

"I need to get...my shirt," muttered Russell.

Raven grabbed the shirt and used it as a handkerchief. A loud, prolonged honk reverberated through the air. The glass lamp tinkled again.

"Never liked the shirt, actually," said Russell. He turned and started to leave.

"About the tat," said Liz, stepping closer.

Keeping one eye on Raven, Russell made a dismissing motion toward his bare chest. "Oh, what's a tattoo with another woman's name when one's life is at stake." He edged closer to the door. "Interesting meeting you. And..." *the Cro-Magnon* "Raven. Really must be going. I have to get back—" he gestured toward the door "—to the planet Earth."

Liz's red mouth curled into a small smile. "You're funny," she said softly. "I like that."

Her eyes—the color of a sun-spangled sea—glistened in a way Charlotte's never had. And Charlotte never looked at him the way Liz did now. Warm. Inviting. Memories teased his senses again: how it felt to submerge his fingers into her silky hair, to breath in her intoxicating perfume...

Before he left her, he had to know something. "Why did you...tattoo me with your name if you belong to—" He nodded at Raven, who dabbed at his nose with Russell's former shirt while staring blankly at the side wall.

She smiled wider. A dimple in her cheek came to life. "Why'd you express undying love for me if *you* belong to..." Instead of finishing her sentence, she gave Russell a knowing look.

"Un-undying love?" he stammered.

"'I crave the stain of tears,'" she quoted, her voice dropping to a husky whisper, "'the aftermark of almost too much love.'"

It was one of his favorite lines from Frost. "I suppose the tattoo came soon after I spouted that?"

She nodded again, her eyes sparkling. "You'd better go before the blood starts flowing into Raven's head again."

Russell took a step toward the door, then stopped. "I guess I won't be back. To get the...tat removed." Much to his surprise, a pang of remorse shot through him.

"No, probably not a good idea. After all, you're getting married in a week. And I'm getting married in a week..." Her voice trailed off.

"Both of us, in a week?"

Their eyes held. The air felt charged, expectant. A burn-

ing need flared within him, and Russell had the crazy
thought that his life would only be half lived without her.

From across the room, Raven grunted something unintelligible.

"Best you go," whispered Liz. "I'll handle Crow." She
winked. "Bet you forgot I'm a poet, too." She smiled, but
not before Russell caught a fleeting sadness in her eyes.

I'm getting married in a week, he reminded himself. *This
whatever-it-is I'm feeling is the aftermath of a Wild Turkey–soaked bachelor party. Time to get going...Charlotte's
waiting.*

He tore himself away from Liz's sea green eyes and left.

Once he hit Hollywood Boulevard, reality engulfed him.
Traffic whizzed by. The stench of exhaust mixed with
scents of French fries and hot dogs. A kid with a blaring
radio skateboarded past. The bright L.A. sun beat down on
his skin.

His skin. He'd almost forgotten he was shirtless.

As though in answer to his prayers, Mr. T-shirt materialized a few feet ahead. Russell fished in his pocket and
extracted a bill. Picking up his speed, he waved it, calling
out, "I'll take one. Any one."

"Knew you'd be back, brother." The vendor's eyes widened as he took the bill. "Twenty? For twenty bucks, you
get—"

"No steak knives. No plates. Just the shirt." Russell
grabbed one off the top of the pile.

"Nice tat, brother. I see Liz is signing her work these
days."

Russell threw the shirt over his head, not wanting to
correct the man that a tattoo wasn't art. Signing "Liz" on
someone's skin wasn't exactly like Toulouse-Lautrec signing an oil painting.

"Your change—"

Russell bounded toward his Honda, parked at the curb.
"Keep it!" he shouted over his shoulder.

As he gunned the motor and peeled away, he heard the

T-shirt vendor yelling, "Your credit's good with me, brother! I owe you three T's!"

"DARLING," cooed Charlotte as she opened the door. Her lips froze mid-coo. "You dressed like *that* to meet Mommy's family?" Her gaze inched upward. "And what happened to your hair?"

Russell glanced over his shoulder. On that last stretch down Beverly Boulevard, he could have sworn he saw two Harleys in his rearview mirror. It was either his rampant paranoia, or Raven and Liz—the lovebirds in leather—were hot on his trail.

"I'll explain later," he said quickly, stepping inside the Madays' foyer and shutting the door closed behind him.

Charlotte's blue eyes frosted over. "Russell, you knew how important today is for me. And you show up—" she straightened her slim shoulders with a dramatic roll "—looking like something from a bargain-basement sale."

He loved her cool style and poise, but he wondered if she was capable of an analogy that didn't involve retail. "Yes, well, let me tame my hair and I'll meet you in the backyard." He charged toward the guest bathroom, ducking in time to miss one of Mrs. Maday's precious art objects, an eighteenth-century Rouen wall fountain that jutted from the wall.

Charlotte followed, her high-heeled sandals clicking across the marble floor. "And that shirt! It looks like something you picked off a street persona—"

"Street person," he corrected, not breaking his pace. "And I didn't pick it, I bought it."

"Rus-sell," called someone in a singsong voice. Mrs. Maday, dressed in a blur of ivory and diamonds, swept across the room toward him, her arms posed in a welcoming gesture. Casual summer attire might mean shorts and swimsuits to the gentry, but jewelry was *de rigueur* for the Madays. Long ago, he had decided they were like the military. Just as three stripes meant something to the army, so did three diamonds to the Madays.

"You're finally here," she said, patting him lightly on his arm. "So sorry to hear about that nasty student with the bad grade." She stopped, a look of horror creasing her powdered face. "Oh, my God. What did he do to you? Charlotte—" she waved a jeweled hand toward her daughter "—your poor husband-to-be had a vicious encounter with that angry student. Have Wendel make him a drink."

"But—"

"Charlotte, do what Mommy says."

Usually Russell deplored these Mommy-Charlotte exchanges, but this one had a refreshing twist in his favor. If everyone thought he'd had a "vicious encounter," it would rationalize his appearance. Explanations about his hair and attire could be explained in two words: "angry student."

"The usual, please," chimed Russell, smiling for the first time since he'd woken up. His headache had subsided to the point where a bit of the hair of the dog sounded good. "Rocks."

Charlotte cut him a we'll-talk-later look before heading toward the glass-paneled doors that offered a view of the garden and guest house.

"Heavens, what did he do?" exclaimed Mrs. Maday, cupping one hand against her cheek as she stared, aghast, at Russell's hair. "Try to pull it out by the roots?"

"Something like that," he muttered. "I'll try to beat it into submission and join you—"

"You must see my new Shenkel," she interrupted, waving her hand toward the garden. "Nineteenth-century, although the curators at the V and A in London say it's very difficult to be one hundred percent certain. The statue, they believe, is modeled after the young beggars of the era..."

Russell nodded, accustomed to Mrs. Maday's chatter about her art acquisitions. A Wild Turkey was definitely in order.

"Russell, my boy." Mr. Maday strolled inside from the garden, his hand outstretched. "Charlotte told me about the altercation with your pupil." He pumped Russell's hand in a male-bonding grip. "Education is a jungle these days.

Schoolrooms are the war zone. Much better when you can channel your career into literary criticism full-time.'' Mr. Maday clapped him on the back and proceeded to lead him outside.

Russell knew this was Charlotte's dream—for him to continue writing his book reviews for the *L.A. Times,* and to eventually parlay that into a career as a successful literary critic. It would sound good on the society pages. Charlotte Harrington and her husband the literary critic, Russell Harrington. Not that he was fighting her plan. Having the security of a profession and a family were paramount to Russell, especially after the way he grew up.

Mr. Maday and Russell passed through the doors and walked down the sloping lawn toward the guests. Russell was contemplating if the grass had been dyed for this party—the color looked like something out of Oz—when Mr. Maday pointed toward a diminutive statue they were passing.

''Mrs. Maday's new Shenkel. Cost forty big ones. Told her to keep it inside, but no, she wanted to display it like some kind of expensive lawn flamingo.''

Russell eyed the gray three-foot statue. If he hadn't been told it was art, he would have thought it was a birdbath. Or an odd-looking ashtray. He hoped everyone at the party was well educated in *objets d'art*; otherwise, the little Shenkel might be decorated in nicotine butts by the end of the party.

''Mrs. Maday went out to buy a dress and returned with this,'' continued Mr. Maday with a chuckle. ''The Maday women,'' he said, lowering his voice in a good-ol'-boy aside, ''spoiled to the core. But that's how we like 'em, eh?'' He winked and clapped Russell on the back again.

Russell forced a smile. Spoiled was Charlotte's middle name—something he hoped would change with their marriage. After all, their agreement was to subsist on his salary, although Charlotte could dip into her trust fund for any personal items. He stared at the stoic features on the Shenkel's face. He hoped grotesque art objects weren't the kind of personal items Charlotte coveted. He tried to dismiss the image of little monster statuettes littering their home.

For a fleeting moment, his mind went back to the waiting room at The Rose Tattoo. Cozy. Inviting. Liz might look like a Hell's Angel groupie, but her decorating tastes veered toward vintage *Leave It to Beaver*. The kind of place a man would want to go home to at night...

"Wendel!" Mr. Maday's baritone voice boomed across the crowded lawn party. "Where's our hero's Wild Turkey?"

Russell straightened and checked out the crowd. The backyard looked like a congregation of white-sale enthusiasts. White shorts, white shoes, white hair. For a moment, Russell felt snow-blind.

Mr. Maday strolled toward one of the groups in white, his hand outstretched. Ready to exercise the male-bonding grip, Russell thought.

"Your drink," Wendel said drolly, materializing out of nowhere. He extended a silver tray, his gaze never lifting to Russell's hair, an admirable show of constraint.

"It's my new look," explained Russell as he slid the glass off the tray. "Called the 'altercation.' All the professors are wearing it these days."

Wendel bowed slightly, but not before Russell caught the corner of the butler's mouth curling upward. In the two years he'd been frequenting the Madays' residence, he'd never seen Wendel lose his reserved demeanor. A slight smile was akin to thunderous applause—and Russell desperately needed any form of approval right now.

"Anything else, sir?"

"Wendel, we've discussed this 'sir' thing before. I haven't been knighted—I'm merely betrothed." He took a quick sip, relishing the bite of bourbon. "Charlotte's not very pleased with my, uh, look today."

"I think another Wild Turkey will lessen the sting," Wendel responded. "I'll bring reinforcements."

As Wendel disappeared into the crowd, Mr. Maday approached, his arm cradling the elbow of a plump middle-aged woman. Her white frothy outfit reminded Russell of a cloud. An earthbound cloud.

"This is Agnes, Mrs. Maday's second cousin," announced Mr. Maday, pulling her closer. "She arrived yesterday from London."

"Jack Nicholson?" she asked, squinting at the front of Russell's T-shirt.

"What?" said Russell.

"Your shirt. It says Jack Nicholson For President."

Russell glanced down. Even upside down he easily read Jack Nicholson For President in blazing red letters. He didn't want to look down at his chest anymore today—every time he did, he found something new there. At least this logo was on his shirt and not his skin.

"Senator from Iowa," he answered glibly before taking another long, smooth sip of the Wild Turkey.

Charlotte eased next to him, coiling her arm through his. "I hope you don't mind if I kidnap my future husband," she simpered, edging him out of earshot of her father and Agnes.

"Take off that shirt," she whispered, guiding Russell through the throng of white. "I don't want people thinking I'm marrying a hippie-actor radical."

"There are no more hippies. They all grew up to be venture capitalists."

"Please, Russell—" She smiled and mouthed "Hello" to someone walking past. Without turning her head back to Russell, she added, "You can wear one of Daddy's polo shirts instead." She twiddled her fingers in a wave to someone else.

"Your father is an extra-extra large. I'll look like a walking pillowcase." *Or worse, like second cousin Agnes.* He felt relieved at the look of consternation on Charlotte's face. He knew he had appealed to her sense of retail logic—it was far better for Russell to wear the right size, even if he did look somewhat odd.

He took a congratulatory sip of Wild Turkey. This wasn't going to be such a bad afternoon, after all. He got to keep the shirt on his back. Wendel would be supplying a fresh drink any moment. Life was good.

"That's the dude!"

Russell nearly choked. "Dude" was not known to the Maday vocabulary. But it was known to...

He turned, stiff spined, and stared in the direction of the yelled words.

A black mountain lurched down the grassy slope toward him. People were parting for its passage, like the Red Sea making way for Moses.

Except it wasn't Moses.

It was Raven.

3

DREAD PERMEATED every cell of Russell's being.

This was not turning into a very good day.

"I think he's heading toward you!" exclaimed Charlotte, her voice leaping into a shrill octave. Her manicured fingernails dug into Russell's arm. "Who is that...degenerate?"

Frantically looking around for an escape, Russell mumbled, "Uh, it's my...student."

Charlotte gasped. Her nails dug in an extra inch. "The one you gave the bad grade?"

Twenty feet away, Raven stopped and jabbed an accusing finger at Russell. "That's the dude with my girl's name on his tat!"

Charlotte focused her wide blue eyes on Russell. "On your what?"

The crowd, as though on cue, all turned and stared at him. Someone muttered, "Is Jack Nicholson running for President?"

Russell would have to think fast to get out of this mess.

"What's that?" he shouted, pointing at the sky.

Raven frowned and looked up. Charlotte loosened her nail grip and did the same.

Russell slid behind a group of Mr. Maday look-alikes. Peering over their white and silvered heads, he saw that Raven was still searching the skies.

Russell skirted the edge of the crowd and headed toward the pool—freedom was as easy as one mad dash around the kidney-shaped lagoon and through the back gate to his parked car.

His feet flew out from underneath him as something jerked hard around his throat.

"I got you now!" yelled Raven, his bulky forearm strangling Russell in a neck hold.

"Oh," squealed a female guest, "the angry student is manhandling Charlotte's fiancé!"

"Die, scumbag," said Raven, his voice an ominous rumble.

Russell grimaced and coughed slightly. *Just my luck,* he thought. *Years of studying literature and the last word I hear is "scumbag."*

A loud, piercing whistle averted the crowd's attention. Raven turned his head toward the sound. Russell slid his gaze past Raven's skull-and-crossbones earring to the top of the sloping lawn.

There stood Liz in her signature formfitting white-leather outfit. Sunlight sparked off her tumble of red hair, making her look like a lighted matchstick.

"Raven, cut the macho theatrics!" she called out, her husky voice carrying over the gasp of the crowd.

"Who-o-o are you?" asked Mrs. Maday, sounding like the caterpillar in *Alice in Wonderland.*

"Raven's, uh, fiancée," Liz answered, glancing quickly at Mrs. Maday before zeroing back on Raven. "Or soon to be *ex*-fiancée if he doesn't stop acting like such a jerk," she added emphatically.

"Ex?" Raven's voice cracked on the single syllable. He looked back at Russell and tightened his hold. "If I lose my girl—"

"Oh, Donald, do something," squealed Mrs. Maday. "That angry student is going to kill Russell!" She began nervously waving her hands like a bird unable to take flight.

Liz had to act. Raven wouldn't hurt a fly—but he might maim a certain professor. *Now.* She broke into a run, tearing across the lawn toward Raven. As she hurdled a low table, Charlotte screamed and clutched her pearl necklace. Liz jumped and landed with a thud on Raven's back...

Time slowed. She clung to his leather jacket as he

swayed from the unexpected load and staggered back several steps. Russell, still clutched in Raven's death grip, struggled before falling hard against him. The impact propelled all three of them toward the pool.

Releasing her hold, Liz rolled onto a patch of grass. An explosion of water told her where Russell and Raven had landed. The crowd screamed.

"Get the life saver!" yelled Mr. Maday to the butler, who hastily crossed over to the other side of the pool.

Raven and Russell—a mass of white, red and black—thrashed about in the water. Whenever Russell's head submerged, the crowd's screams intensified.

Looking around, Liz grabbed what looked to be a water-boy birdbath. It was surprisingly light, so she carried it to the pool's edge. Tracking Raven's head, she carefully raised the birdbath and waited for the right moment. When Raven came whooshing up from the water, she brought the object down forcefully. A chunk of the water boy's head went flying off into the deep end, accompanied by Mrs. Maday's shrill cry. "My Shenkel!"

Raven stopped and stared straight ahead. Then his eyes rolled back in his head and he crumpled into Russell's arms.

"Good Lord," gasped Russell, spitting water and grappling with the unexpected mass of deadweight. "Someone help me!"

Mr. Maday jumped into the pool, Italian loafers and all. Several men followed suit. Into the mass of flailing, swimming and bumbling, the butler tossed the life saver, which floated idly past the men as they hoisted Raven out of the water.

Liz overheard snippets of conversation trickle through the crowd. "Russell gave him an F, I hear." "Well, no wonder—did you see how he spells 'Mother' on his shirt?" "Jack Nicholson For President? Who's his running mate? Warren Beatty?"

Panting, she set the birdbath back down and scanned the throng of Bel Air–ites, wondering how Russell found these people. Maybe one of those personal ads. "Pompous, emptyheaded socialites seeking intellectual diversion." Russell seemed...too good for these upper-crust types. *Bet I understand the symbolism of Yeats better than any of these blue bloods.* The thought gave her a small surge of satisfaction.

She looked back at Raven, sopping wet in his black-leather outfit, being held up by Mr. Maday and three of his drenched cronies. Russell, the tattoo faintly visible underneath his soaked Jack Nicholson T-shirt, had slumped into a nearby lawn chair.

"I think you and Rabid should go," announced Mrs. Maday, suddenly standing next to Liz.

"Raven."

"What?"

"His name's Raven. And we'll be happy to leave...I'll just need some help carting him outside."

Mrs. Maday tipped her head to one side. "How did you get here?"

"On our hogs."

Mrs. Maday sucked in a breath of air, which caused her chest to puff out. "They rode in on beasts," she said, her voice rising shakily. "I should have known."

Raven grunted and lurched to his feet. The crowd shrank back. One woman yelled, "The student with the bad grade is coming back to life!"

Liz rolled her eyes before leveling a look at Russell. "Can you help me get him into your car? We'll drive him to my place."

"I'll drive him?" asked Russell incredulously, straightening in his chair. "What happens when he comes to and I'm driving along the Santa Monica Freeway? I'm not very good at steering the car and fighting off strangulation at the same time."

Liz coaxed Raven to his feet. "I'll sit with him in the back seat. I know it's hard to believe, but deep down he's a pussycat."

"How deep? Two miles?"

Liz flashed Russell a cut-the-act look. "Just give me a hand, and cool it, okay?"

Charlotte huddled at the edge of the crowd. "Russell, darling, don't get near that heathen."

"Don't worry, Char," he answered, his voice heavy with irony, "he's a pussycat."

"No," she fumed, "I mean *her*."

"Get under his left arm," instructed Liz, ignoring Charlotte. "Okay, and up we go."

They lifted Raven to his feet and began walking him slowly through the throng of people, who patted Russell while murmuring words of encouragement.

Upon reaching his car, Liz fumed, "Now that we're alone, I'd like to know why everyone treated you as though you were going into battle, maybe never to return."

Balancing Raven with one hand, Russell opened the back door. "They probably think I'm in the midst of some war between the powers of dark and light. Your fiancé representing the dark side, of course." He guided a woozy Raven into the back seat.

"Like some Stephen King novel," she responded with a huff. "Didn't know these rich types read that kind of stuff."

Russell headed around the car to the driver's side. "Only when they're forced to. It's a form of popular-fiction therapy for the literati."

Their eyes met over the top of the car. His twinkled with amusement, the first lighthearted reaction she'd seen from him all day. She tried to avoid his eyes, but they snagged her with their good humor. A corner of his lip curled up and she thought, for one dizzying moment, that he was the sexiest man she'd ever seen.

But damned if she'd let him know that.

"And that one woman thinks we ride beasts," she added, getting in the last word. "I'll have you know my *beast* placed first at both Biketoberfest and the regional HOG Rally." She slid into the back seat next to Raven and slammed shut her door.

As Russell drove through the winding Bel Air streets, she looked at the manicured lawns, ornate gates and picture-perfect homes. "So this is going to be your life, huh?"

"What?" Russell turned down the classical music on his radio.

She tapped the window, indicating what lay outside. "Stepford High Society. A world of nonwrinkling fabrics and skin."

After a pause, he said, "'Wisdom outweighs any wealth.'"

"So says you."

"So said Sophocles, actually." He sneezed. "Excuse me."

"Better take off that wet T-shirt," she offered. "You'll catch cold."

He eased to a halt at a Stop sign, pulled off the shirt and tossed it onto the seat next to him.

"We'll get your pants off when we get to my place."

"That's really not necessary."

"I meant that literally, not figuratively." She caught his disbelieving look in the rearview mirror. "What's the matter? Didn't think I knew what 'figuratively' meant?"

He shook his head. "No. That's not what I was thinking."

"You thought I was propositioning you?"

He stretched his neck from side to side, as though he suddenly needed to work out a kink. "Really, Liz, I didn't think—"

"If I'm interested in a guy, and he's interested in me, then I let things progress. Know what I mean? Just because I do tats, wear leather and drive a Harley doesn't mean I don't follow courting rituals."

She heard the edge in her voice, but she didn't care. This was the guy who thought she branded men like some kind of desperate cowgirl. Besides, being dipped into that bizarre Bel Air party scene reminded her of being a new kid, the "different" kid, at school. An experience she repeated every few months while growing up. In the carnivals and fairs where her dad ran his own tat shop, she had an extended family that consisted of carny folk. But in public schools she kept to herself, never fitting in with the pretty, popular girls in crisply ironed dresses and shiny hair pinned back with barrettes.

She avoided the rearview mirror because she knew he was glancing at her, analyzing her reaction. Just as he had done last night, in between spouting poetry and kissing her.

Kissing her. Heat skittered across her skin as she remembered the velvet sensation of his lips pressed against hers.

She rolled down the window, hoping some fresh air would cool her hot thoughts. "Turn left here," she said, forcing herself to sound levelheaded, detached. Or so she hoped. "And take Sunset to Vermont. My apartment's near there."

Twenty minutes later, they were guiding a very wobbly kneed Raven into Liz's place. Russell was familiar with these Hollywood apartment buildings, remnants of a bygone era's architecture. Peeling stucco, dried-up courtyards, tiled roofs. Supposedly the studios built these small complexes in the twenties and thirties to house their contract actors.

"This way to the bedroom," said Liz, panting, as she tilted her head toward a hallway. "We'll peel off his duds and tuck him in." She smothered a groan. "Getting this wet leather off him is going to be worse than skinning a moose."

"Unfortunately, this moose is still alive and kicking," muttered Russell. "Let's hope he doesn't wake up and take offense. Again."

They staggered into the bedroom and heaved Raven onto the bed. The bedsprings creaked and groaned under his weight. He grunted and stared bleary-eyed at the ceiling.

Liz clapped her hands. "Okay, Russell, let's start skinning."

Later, Russell stood in the middle of her living room, stretching his arms over his head. "Good Lord. This must be how trappers felt after a rough day at work."

Liz sashayed past him toward the front door. "I'm going to my neighbor's—he's about your size—and borrow a pair of pants."

"You're not going to bring him back to 'skin' me as well, are you?"

She stopped and cocked her head. "That's a joke, right?"

"Partially."

She turned and crossed to him with careful, stealthy steps. Images of being stalked by a jungle animal colored Russell's thoughts. A very sexy jungle animal.

"After we skin you," she said in a silky voice, "we're going to roll you up with herbs and cheese and bake you at three-fifty for an hour. What do you think of that?"

"Skinless," he said, forcing air into his words. "Very healthy."

She stopped right in front of him and stood spread-eagled, her hands on her hips. "And good for the heart." She winked seductively, turned and left.

Russell released a pent-up breath and stared at the open door, listening to her retreating footsteps.

"Here I am," he murmured, "bare chested in the living room of Sheena, Queen of the Jungle, after peeling forty tons of leather off Raven, King of the Beasts." He rubbed his temples with his fingers. "There's only one explanation. I've stepped into an alternative universe."

He looked around the room. An alternative universe that featured pictures of Faulkner, Steinbeck, and Elizabeth Barrett Browning hung here and there. Bookcases lined two walls, crammed with novels. He felt slightly chagrined. Hardly the barbaric atmosphere he'd expected. It seemed Sheena enjoyed literature. Read it, revered it. Unlike Charlotte who, along with her family, raised money for cultural ventures—such as the university's new library wing—yet she didn't seem to like opening a book and losing herself in it.

"Success for Liz's scavenger hunt!" exclaimed Liz, waving a pair of black leather pants as she traipsed back into the room. "George, my next-door neighbor—and aspiring horror novelist, by the way—has offered these." She tossed them to Russell, who caught them midair. "They should fit—or I'm not a good judge of men's buns."

Russell felt heat flare up his chest to his face. "Well, uh, thank you. An-and George." He held the pants in front of him. "If you wouldn't mind…"

She arched one eyebrow, then formed an O of understanding with those red lips. "Privacy. Of course. Let me close the front door." She did. "And I'll go freshen up in the bathroom while you change." She started to exit the living room, then stopped. Looking over her shoulder, she added, "I didn't feel comfortable asking to borrow a pair of underwear."

"I'm glad you didn't."

"I'd offer a pair of my—"

"No." His gaze dropped to her fanny, where he saw no tell-tale panty lines around that curvaceous bottom. Did she even wear anything under those sprayed-on pants? The thought of her bare skin made his groin tighten. He tried to assume a nonchalant pose. "Besides, I don't think they'd fit."

"I have some stretchy lace—"

"No." He swallowed and tried to wet his suddenly dry mouth. Images of stretchy black lace hugging Liz's derriere floated through his thoughts.

"It's cool. Just don't play proper and wear those wet…boxers or whatever you wear…under those dry pants. You'll be uncomfortable."

He shifted his stance, not wanting her to see how uncomfortable he was already after that stretchy-lace comment. "I'll take that into consideration."

"Take it into con…?" She sighed dramatically. "Do I have to stand here and make sure you strip to the buff?"

The thought of being naked with this wild woman pushed him over the edge. Every synapse, even those he had numbed after last night's Wild Turkey overdose, suddenly flared to life. Every adolescent fantasy he'd ever had about being with a woman congealed into one bright white-hot core meltdown in the center of his brain as he imagined what he'd do, and what she'd do.

"Well, do I?" she asked again.

"I hope so." He caught his breath. "I mean, uh, no. No, you don't have to stand there." A trickle of sweat broke loose from his hairline. He pretended to scratch his head while flicking the itching drip.

She flashed him a quizzical look. "Are you all right?"

"No. I mean yes." He raised his eyebrows. "I'm just waiting for you to leave." *So I can stem this hormone tide.*

"Okay, I'll be back in a few minutes."

He nodded. As soon as he heard the bathroom door click shut, he whipped off his wet pants and boxers. Naked, he juggled the wet mass of clothes. He couldn't toss them on the floor. Or leave them on the couch.

Against the wall next to the front door was a small dining table with two chairs. He crossed to it. Pulling out a chair, he neatly draped his pants over the top rung. He bent over to fold his boxers over the bottom rung when, from behind him, he heard the front door open.

"Oh, my heavens!" trilled an elderly female voice.

He squeezed his eyes shut.

His stomach plummeted like a broken elevator.

He was mooning a little old lady.

Mustering the last dregs of dignity, he pivoted around, clutching his boxers over his privates.

She looked to be in her seventies. Dressed in a prim pink suit and gripping a small matching pink handbag, she stood stiffly before him. Her small blue eyes darted down his physique, then quickly back up.

"You—" her voice wavered on the single word "—must be Elizabeth's fiancé."

He almost dropped his boxers.

"That's right, Auntie," Liz chimed in from somewhere behind him, "this is my fiancé, Russell."

He slid a look over his shoulder. Liz stood several feet behind him.

"Play along," she mouthed. Her gaze dipped down and up, and she flashed him an A-OK sign.

Next I'll be branded USDA Choice, he thought. He slowly sat down, trying not to wince as his bare bottom met the cool vinyl seat.

"Auntie, let's leave Russell alone for a moment so he can get dressed." Liz strolled past and playfully trailed a finger along his shoulder. Her touch burned a path across his skin. He bunched the boxers in his lap, not wanting Auntie to see more than she already had.

Easing Auntie out the front door, Liz murmured in that Lauren Bacall voice, "Hon, I'm going to show Auntie my garden. Your brother's resting in the other room, reading some magazines—"

Russell almost stood, but stopped himself. "I thought *brother* was out. As in cold," he said quickly.

"He was out cold. But now he's coming to." She cupped Auntie's elbow and started to step outside.

"Uh-h-h-h," said Russell loudly, all the while thinking he had never in his life made a sound like a stuck car horn.

In unison, Liz and Auntie stopped and looked at him.

"Is he sitting on something?" asked Auntie, looking perplexedly at Liz.

Russell ignored the comment. With his free hand, he stabbed his thumb in the direction of the bedroom. "I hope brother doesn't get up too soon. You know how cranky he can get after he's been sleeping." *Or how cranky he'll get if he finds me naked in his fiancée's living room.*

"He's absorbed in his favorite magazine," said Liz offhandedly. "Trust me, he's staying put." She lowered her voice to Auntie. "Russell loves his family. Always worrying about them."

Russell toyed with the idea of blowing Liz's cover. Demanding she stay put until he got dressed and out of this Alice-down-the-rabbit-hole world.

He opened his mouth to speak, then stopped when Auntie glanced his way. Her blue eyes twinkled and her lips curved into a benevolent smile reminiscent of Mother Teresa's.

"Bless you, Russell. A family man." Her eyes misted over and she swiped at a corner of her eye. "After all Elizabeth's been through," she murmured. She smiled and raised her voice. "I hoped and prayed she'd find a husband like you."

"Auntie," said Liz softly. "Let's go outside—Russell needs some privacy."

"Oh!" exclaimed Auntie, looking quickly away. "I forgot he was...well, you know."

"Hurry back," said Russell glumly as the door closed.

"How many other men go to their bachelor party and end up engaged to two women," he muttered, leaping to his feet and stepping into the black leather pants. He pulled them up, but they stopped somewhere midthigh. Too tight. He sucked in his stomach and gave the pants an upward heave. Magically, they slipped over his hips. "Wonderful. I'm encased in a leather girdle," he said, afraid to breathe.

He yanked on the zipper, praying it would make it to the top—

"What the hell you doin' here?" boomed a baritone voice behind him.

Russell froze. But only for a moment. He raced to the door and flung it open, ready to charge outside.

There stood Liz and Auntie, bending over a barrel filled with bunches of leafy basil.

"Hon, leaving already?" asked Liz. Auntie turned and graced him with another saintly smile.

"Brother's up," said Russell quickly.

"Lovely!" exclaimed Auntie, enthusiasm filling her voice. She patted Liz on the arm. "I get to meet your fiancé's side of the family." With an exuberance that defied her years, Auntie stepped briskly past Russell and into the room.

Liz followed. Taking Russell's arm, she gently steered him back inside. "Trust me," she whispered.

Raven stood in front of the hallway entrance, naked except for the women's magazine he held in front of him. A model in a bikini graced the cover. Above her frothy hairdo was the heading, "How To Keep Your Cool When Temperatures Soar."

Auntie's back stiffened. Her voice slid up an octave as she said, "My word. Do these boys belong to a family of nudists?"

Raven glanced from Auntie to Liz. "This is Auntie?"

Liz nodded. From where he stood, Russell thought he caught her flashing Raven a don't-blow-it-for-me look.

"Nice meeting you, ma'am. I'm, uh, Raven."

Russell wondered if the blow to Raven's head had triggered a takeover by another personality. Maybe this was the pussycat personality Liz had alluded to earlier. If so, now was the time to make a speedy exit before kitty metamorphosed back into a roaring lion.

Russell snapped his fingers as though he just remembered something. "Almost forgot! I have an appointment—urgent appointment—with—" he looked around the room, his gaze landing on the portrait of Faulkner "—with William. Dr. William. Nasty intestinal thing." He patted his stomach as though to indicate the exact location. "Sorry to dress and run..." He veered toward the front door.

"Russell," said Liz silkily, blocking his exit. "Don't go yet. Auntie wants to take our picture."

"Can't it wait?" he said through clenched teeth. "Dr. William—"

"—called and rescheduled your appointment for three this afternoon. Sorry, hon, I forgot to mention it earlier." Liz's eyes twinkled mischievously. "You have time to spare."

He glanced down at his tight leather pants and bare chest. Shrugging apologetically to Auntie, he said, "What a shame I'm not properly dressed." He tried not to sound too chipper. "But if I head home now, I can grab some suitable clothes before my doctor's appointment and return later to have our picture taken." *Much* later.

Auntie shook her head, smiling all the while. "No, son. It's the first time we've met—having your picture taken now is a good omen. Let's step outside again while Rover gets dressed.''

"Raven," Liz corrected.

"Absolutely," said Auntie, heading toward the door.

Outside, Russell and Liz stood close to each other while Auntie, several feet down the concrete walkway, adjusted the lens on her camera.

"A good omen?" he asked quietly, eyeing Auntie.

"She's superstitious. Long story. Has to do with her first and only love."

"Speaking of love, care to explain why you introduced me as your fiancé?" Then he mumbled to himself. "And why I agreed to this charade?"

Liz eased her arm around his waist and flashed him a loving smile, obviously for Auntie's benefit. "If I marry by my twenty-seventh birthday, which is this Saturday," she whispered, "Auntie signs over my trust fund. And you agreed because you're a nice guy and don't like to hurt little old ladies' feelings."

Plus it was damn difficult to remain enraged with a honey-voiced temptress gripping your waist and whispering in that husky, Lauren Bacall come-hither voice. "Twenty-seventh birthday," he muttered, trying to keep his mind focused. "Another superstition?"

"You're quick."

"But why force yourself to marry someone—"

Her small hand tightened around his waist. "It's always been my dream to go to college, get a degree in English literature, then write or teach. It's really important to me."

His mouth dropped open. If more English teachers looked like her, the illiteracy rate in this country would disappear. "You write...?"

"Sonnets. I know I look like a biker babe, but inside I'm Elizabeth Barrett Browning. Remember?"

Auntie peeked over her camera. "Okay, you two love-birds, say 'we can't wait to get married.'"

Russell blinked at the poised lens. "I can't believe this is happening."

Liz snuggled closer under his arm, molding herself to his side. Her body heat was like a match to a fuse. Small internal fires blasted to life within him as he remembered the taste of her lips and how she softly moaned his name...

Auntie hesitated briefly. "Sorry. Forgot to release this thingamajig. Hold that pose a few moments longer."

Russell looked down at Liz. Wisps of her hair curled provocatively along her cheek. She seemed to sense his gaze as her eyes lifted to meet his.

He didn't like how good, how exciting, it felt to be near her. Yet he didn't want to move from her side. "Shouldn't we confess—let Auntie know Raven is really your fiancé?" he asked quietly, all the while struggling with his own guilt.

Liz nestled closer, liking how he flinched. Lightly tickling her fingers against his bare skin, she whispered, "He's not my fiancé."

"Not? Has anybody bothered to tell him?"

"I needed someone to pose as my fiancé, that's all. Unfortunately, Raven's been taking his role a little too seriously."

"A little? I'd hate to see what 'a lot' is."

"One," crooned Auntie, peering through the camera's viewer.

Liz inhaled his woodsy cologne. Her insides tingled as she recalled nuzzling close and drowning in that familiar scent.

"Two," said Auntie.

He turned his head, his gaze catching hers. In that moment, something fired between them. Unspoken. Powerful. She raised her chin slightly, remembering how his kiss had left her aching for more...

He seemed to hesitate, then his lips descended to her mouth.

"Three," chirped Auntie. The camera snapped.

RUSSELL UNLOCKED his apartment door, grateful to be home again. No sooner had he stepped inside than the phone began ringing.

He crossed to the dining room and grabbed the receiver off the wall phone. "Don't ask," he answered in anticipation of Drake's question.

There was a cool moment of silence. "Ask what?" Charlotte's voice could freeze-dry coffee. "Ask something like, why did you ruin today's party?"

Another chilling moment passed. "I'm sorry," he said, glancing down at the leather pants that looked as though they'd been shrink-wrapped around the bottom half of his body. "Please accept my apology." She didn't even know about the tattoo yet.

"Mommy's very upset about her Shenkel."

"Her what?"

"Her Shenkel. The statue."

"Oh. Yes, of course. The statue."

"That...that...angry student's moll used it as though it were a bat."

Moll? "It must be insured," he offered.

"That's not the point," she snapped. "The statue is one of a kind. And now it's ruined."

"It'll make a great conversation piece. At future parties, we'll gather around it and discuss the day the Shenkel doubled as a bat."

"Not amusing, Russell." He heard her inhale slowly. It was her cue that she had something important to say. "I want you to meet Mommy's family tonight for dinner. We've made reservations at Chez Nous. Seven p.m. It'll be an opportunity for them to meet the *real* you."

Versus the barbarian they all met today, he thought. "I'll be there."

"With matching socks."

He bit his lip so as not to laugh. If Charlotte saw him now, the last thing she'd care about would be whether he wore matching socks.

"Matching. Definitely," he said, trying to sound somber.

He'd no sooner hung up the phone than there was a loud knocking at the door. He started to answer it, then stopped. What if brother Raven had followed him home?

"Who is it?" he called through the door.

"Drake. And since when do you ask?"

Since meeting Raven, Russell thought, swinging the door open.

Drake jumped back, his eyes wide with horror. "Yowza, buddy, what happened?"

Russell stepped back, motioning for Drake to come inside. "I got kidnapped by a hard-rock band."

Drake gave his head a shake, then walked in, looking Russell up and down. "Let me guess. Mötley Crüe wants you to be their poster boy?"

Russell shut the door. "You wouldn't believe me if I told you."

Drake stood in the middle of the room, his gaze glued to Russell's pants. "Buddy, I'd believe *anything* you told me right now."

Russell crossed his arms over his chest. "I'm engaged."

Drake raised his hands in a so-what gesture. "What else is new?"

"No, I'm engaged to the biker babe."

Drake's eyebrows rose slowly. "Uh-huh." His gaze rested on the tattoo on Russell's chest. "And her name's Liz."

"Right. She's also engaged to a mother of a cretin named Raven."

"The plot thickens."

Russell walked over to a chair, sat down and started to cross his leg over his knee. He stopped midmotion, the tight leather prohibiting further movement. "Rock stars must be masochists," he said, setting his foot back down.

"Speaking of starring," he continued, cocking one eyebrow at Drake. "Raven and I were the main attraction at the Madays' pool party."

Drake nodded. "Which, I suppose, explains why you're wearing this stunning new leather outfit."

"Yes."

Drake rolled his eyes. "Does…Liz's family know you're engaged?"

"Her auntie does. She took our picture."

"Uh-huh. I see you had your hair done for the occasion."

"It goes with my new look," Russell said drolly.

"Does Charlotte know you're engaged to Liz?"

"No, I thought I'd wait for her next family party to make that announcement." Russell swore under his breath and stood up. Pacing the room, he began gesturing madly. "In less than twenty-four hours, my life has mutated into some kind of degenerate Hollywood film! Look at me!" He waved his hands at his body. "I look like a reject from *The Rocky Horror Picture Show*."

"Reject, never. Understudy, maybe."

Russell rubbed his thumb along his jaw. "What time is it?"

Drake flicked his wrist and checked his watch. "Almost five. Why?"

"At seven I'm due for dinner at Chez Nous to make amends to Charlotte's family."

"Chez Nous? You can't go dressed like that." Drake smiled slyly. "Unless, of course, you wear a tie."

4

"YOU WERE LIP-LOCKIN'" with that dude again," Raven grumbled. His face was frozen in a look of dark disapproval. Only his Fu Manchu mustache twitched.

He sat in the middle of Liz's bed, her bright daisy-patterned bedspread covering his lower region. When she didn't respond right away, he crossed his massive arms over his naked chest and flexed his biceps. The colorful iguana tattoo slithered.

Liz bit the inside of her lip. The crawling-iguana trick might intimidate others, but she found it amusing. Mostly because his macho theatrics were seriously undermined by the flowery bedspread he sat under.

She cleared her throat, hoping the sound muffled some unsuppressed laughter. "Spying on me?"

"We are engaged, y'know." His angry look dissolved into hurt. The Fu Manchu mustache drooped.

"In name only."

"But we're getting hitched."

"It's a formality."

"I thought we was goin' to Vegas. Nothin' fancy."

"I didn't mean formal. I meant…" She sighed. Raven might have the body of a moose and the attitude of a bouncer, but he had the heart of a child. His heavy-lidded eyes glistened with undisguised pain. Although his sweetness made her ache inside, she had to be honest.

She made an apologetic gesture. "I meant that our getting married is…a convenience. We discussed this. I need to be married to get my trust fund. And that trust fund means my future"—*my dream of getting an education*—

"which is the only reason I asked you to marry me." Her voice softened. "But we're friends, Raven, not lovers. You know that."

"You might learn to love me. With time…" He uncrossed his arms and dropped them to his sides.

Without saying it, he had confessed his love for her. Until this moment, she hadn't realized the depth of his feelings. He had seemed a friend, a pal. Someone who liked to hang out at The Rose Tattoo, watching out for her and playing big brother. Sometimes, on weekends, they'd take their Harleys out for a spin on the long stretch of highway to Palm Springs. She should have realized that to Raven, cruising the freeways and talking tats bordered on courtship.

She offered a sincere smile. "I do love you. As a best buddy. And as we agreed, we'll get divorced in a year. It's not *that* kind of marriage, you know."

"Yeah, I know," he said with a loud sigh. His fingers traced one of the flowers on the cover. "But you told Auntie you're marryin' the teacher dude."

"Yeah, well…" She had a lovely little problem brewing. When her auntie walked in on Russell buck-naked, it just seemed wise to agree with her presumption that he was Liz's fiancé. If she had said the nude man was some guy she had met only the night before, she might as well have kissed that trust fund goodbye.

"What's she gonna think when you marry his brother— me—instead?"

"That I'm fickle?" She laughed. Or tried to. It sounded more like a gurgle. She rubbed her suddenly moist palms together. "It's cool. She'll never know exactly who I'm marrying because she's leaving day after tomorrow for a gloxinia convention."

Raven sat up, his eyes wide. "Is she okay?"

Liz waited a beat before answering. "Gloxinia is a type of plant. Auntie's health is fine. Anyway, because of this convention, she can't make the Vegas wedding. Even if she could, I doubt she'd trek all the way out to Vegas—gambling and neon aren't her things.''

Or so Liz hoped. Intertwining her fingers, she stared at some dried roses that hung, suspended by a yellow ribbon, in the corner. *That'll be me,* she thought. *Hung out to dry if I don't have this wedding-plan thing down pat.*

"After I get married," she continued, needing more to hear her thoughts out loud than to make an explanation to Raven, "the wedding certificate goes to Auntie's lawyer, who confirms I'm married. The trust fund then gets signed over to me."

A quizzical expression creased Raven's face. "Won't the legal dude see my name on the certificate?"

"Yeah. But by then I'll be married, and that's all that matters."

She felt a twinge of remorse that she was deceiving her auntie, but it wasn't an act of malice. She knew Auntie had worried about her since her dad's—Auntie's brother's—death eleven years ago. But this gotta-be-married-to-have-the-trust-fund idea wasn't simply a ploy to make Liz settle down. It was mostly part of Auntie's superstitious bent that true happiness would elude Liz if she didn't marry by her twenty-seventh birthday.

But she couldn't marry on someone else's deadline. True love would arrive someday, but until then, Liz would better herself through a higher education. But a college degree cost money—money she didn't have. The trust fund was to buy Liz her dream—not buy her a husband. She had tried to explain this to Auntie once, but dear ol' Auntie, herself a spinster, refused to believe that matrimony wasn't more important than an education.

Liz fidgeted with the beaded fringe on her top. Nevertheless, lying and juggling were not her style. She'd be glad when the wedding was over, the trust fund was hers and she was enrolled in college.

She'd also be glad when Russell was out of her life. Being attracted to an almost-married man was also not her style. Damn. Why did he have to kiss her again? Just when the picture snapped, too. That moment was now caught on film for all time. Absently, she touched the edge of her mouth, remembering the pressure of his kiss, the texture of his warm lips against hers…

"How long I gotta stay in bed?" asked Raven gruffly.

Rousted from her memory, she glanced around the room, half-glad not to think any more about the sexy English professor.

Her gaze landed on Raven's wet leather ensemble, which was draped strategically across her wicker chair. "At least until your pants dry enough for you to wear them."

He squinted at the bedspread, then around the room. "I feel stupid sittin' in the middle of this petunia blanket. Can't you borrow somethin' for me to put on?"

"I doubt if anyone in this neighborhood—" *or the world* "—is your size, so either you leave here naked, or you stay put. And they're not petunias, they're daisies."

"Same thing," he said. He frowned at the bedspread. "I'll take my chances, then—"

"No you don't," she announced in her end-of-discussion voice. "You aren't walking out of my apartment naked. I don't think Auntie's heart could withstand any more male anatomy today." She flicked her wrist and checked the time. "She and I need to pick up some groceries. Need anything?"

"Maybe—" he looked out the curtained window, avoiding her eyes "—maybe more of those magazines…"

"Magazines?"

"Yeah, uh, you know." He slid a glance to a magazine on the floor. On its cover, a bouffant-haired model smiled toothily.

"Oh. You want one of those…?"

"One with more recipes," he said quickly. Then, lowering his voice to a gravelly, macho range, he added, "Or one of those karate or chopper magazines. Whatever." He rolled his shoulders in an exaggerated masculine impersonation of what she assumed was Sylvester Stallone.

She nodded and crossed to the door. "Recipes. Or karate or choppers. Got it."

But before she shut the door behind her, Raven called out, "Might as well make it one of them recipe ones. After all, I'm gonna be a married man soon."

"YOU'RE GOING TO BE a married man soon, buddy. To more than one lady, too." Drake wiggled his eyebrows. "You're going to need a good day planner to keep track of everyone's birthdays, sizes, anniversaries—"

"You think this is easy for me?" Russell interrupted, stalking across his living room. He stopped upon catching his reflection in a mirror. "Good Lord. Why bother wearing pants? Next time I'll just spray-paint the lower half of my body." He frowned. "Do me a favor?"

"I'm fresh out of spray paint."

"Call The Rose Tattoo and leave a message that—"

"No way, buddy. Last time I called somewhere and left one of your messages, you ended up looking like this. Another of my phone calls and you'll end up with a pierced nose, half an ear and insist I call you Gorgo."

Russell paused a beat before speaking. "You should have gone into engineering. Your imagination is getting the better of you."

"And Ms. Harley has gotten the better of you."

Looking into the mirror, Russell saw the heart tattoo and the name within it. Liz. Elizabeth. She was both names, really. Liz was fiery, snappy, wild. Elizabeth was poetic, creative, thought-provoking. Hell, he wasn't engaged to two women. He was engaged to three.

"What're you thinking, Russ?" Drake appeared behind him, catching his gaze in the mirror.

"I've never been a ladies' man," Russell said with resignation.

"Guess your lover-karma caught up to you."

"I'm serious, Drake."

"Me too. And I'm jealous. You got two great ones, buddy. Grace Kelly and Ann-Margret."

"Ice and fire."

"Mild and wild."

"Good & Plenty."

Drake grinned. "I'd take Plenty, if I were you. But I guess you're more the Good kinda guy."

Russell knew what he meant. Charlotte—Good—was a perfect match for him: lovely, cultured, sophisticated. People often said they looked like the perfect couple. Like those porcelain figures on a wedding cake, he mused. He glanced into the mirror one last time before turning away. Well, not dressed like this, of course. At this moment he hardly looked like a groom. More like the winner of an Alice Cooper look-alike contest.

The kinda guy who would ride off on the back of a Harley driven by Plenty.

Russell raked his hand through his hair, wincing when his fingers got stuck in the mass. "I have to get ready. Practice my speech. I'm going to lose Grace Kelly unless I turn in an Academy Award performance tonight." He knew Drake the theater professor would relate to the Hollywoodisms.

"Buddy, I don't envy you." Drake headed to the door. "Charlotte may not be my taste, but she's dripping with class. And sophistication. And diamonds. Perfect for you, really."

"Hardly the diamonds—"

"Buddy, face it. You're marrying into money. Lots of it."

They'd had this conversation before. It irked Russell that Drake thought Charlotte's wealth was a priority. He was marrying the woman, not her bank account. "Money doesn't keep you warm at night."

"Does if you burn it."

"I meant it doesn't warm your heart and soul. Only a human being can do that."

"You're choking me up, Russ." Drake sighed dramatically and thumped his heart. "If I'd met a nice-looking chick—uh, lady—like Charlotte and then discovered her family vacationed at Fort Knox, I'd have no doubt that a little extra spending cash could keep me warm at night.''

"Spoken by a true cad.''

Drake cocked one eyebrow. "I could love for money.''

"Then move to Italy and be a gigolo.''

Drake winced. "I couldn't perform on command.''

"Strange confession for a man who went into the theater.'' Russell laughed good-naturedly. "I know you, Drake. You love women. Their bodies *and* their minds. You'd rather die than be bound to some rich woman who doesn't get your jokes.''

Drake nodded, suddenly somber. "Can you imagine? I'd be reduced to Henny Youngman one-liners. Worse, knock-knock jokes.''

Russell laughed. "Okay, enough said. When I met Charlotte at the opening of the new library wing, I had no idea she was connected to the Madays. I fell for her smile. Her style. She said she fell for the same.''

Drake looked Russell up and down. "Good thing she's not here. She might have fallen for your style then, but she'd fall into a deep faint at the sight of you now.'' He winked. "Seriously, buddy, you two appreciate the finer things in life—culture, literature, the Ritz. You'll raise beautiful children, adorn the society pages and eventually have immaculate matching plots at Forest Lawn...or wherever your in-laws are.'' He gave a small shiver of dread. "I suppose the good life has its price—eternity next to the Madays.'' He grinned. "If you need moral support, don't call me.'' He reached for the doorknob, paused and looked back over his shoulder. "I'll call The Rose Tattoo and say...?''

"That she can pick up these leather pants...no, that I'll drop them by her business tomorrow. Whatever you do, don't tell her where I live. Raven might overhear. And I'd like for Raven to be nevermore.''

"Got it,'' said Drake. "Pants. Her place. No bird men.''

"Something like that.''

"Give me a buzz later. Let me know if the Ice Princess

thawed.'' Drake shut the door behind him, chortling something about Good & Plenty.

Russell glanced at the clock on the wall. Five-thirty. He could get to Chez Nous, a chic new restaurant in the Palisades, in fifteen minutes. Which gave him ample time to strip, shower and put on something presentable. He shifted his gaze to the mirror. Of course, making his hair behave was a whole other story.

His glance dipped again to the tattoo.

Liz.

He remembered her pliant lips under his. She might look like a Hell's Angel groupie, but she kissed like a prom-night princess. All soft and sweet. He licked his lips, savoring the memory of her honeyed mouth and the soft little moan that escaped her when he pulled away....

''Liz,'' he whispered, tracing the outline of the heart. He remember their standing close, posing for Auntie's camera. It had felt so...*natural* to be close to Liz, to tuck her small body next to his. They had fitted together like two pieces of a puzzle. Snugly. Effortlessly. No wonder Auntie had bought their lie—hell, during those too-brief moments when their bodies touched, even *they* bought their lie.

Or was it a lie?

Insane thought. He rolled his shoulders as though to dislodge the idea. Soul mates were a literary contrivance at best. Hardly a real-life phenomenon.

But Liz had experienced something, too. He remembered the look in her eyes as their gaze held. Deep within those green depths, he had recognized a yearning that mirrored his own. As though their chance encounter had opened a door to something that had eluded them all their lives...

Charlotte. Dinner. Marriage.

He straightened and leveled a sobering look at his reflection. ''Enough with the Liz fantasies,'' he told his reflection, as though it were an evil twin leading him astray. ''You don't need a hot shower—you need to be dunked in a vat of ice cubes.'' One spin on a Harley did not a soul mate make. He was getting last-minute wedding jitters, that was all. Charlotte was his partner, his future wife. End of story.

Turning briskly, he headed toward the bathroom.

His thoughts fell in line with his long, determined strides. Elizabeth—Liz—was like fire. Stand too close and he'd get burned. For a hundred reasons, Charlotte was his ideal mate.

He shoved back the shower curtain and turned on the water. Resisting the urge to turn it to Arctic cold, he adjusted the water's temperature as he began itemizing Charlotte's attributes.

She was organized, which complemented his own logical side. She loved books. Okay, she didn't read them—a small technicality—but she loved them all the same. After all, her family had spearheaded the drive to save a campus historical building and renovate it into a much-needed library. She played a mean game of tennis...

He sucked in his stomach and pulled down the zipper on the leather pants. How many reasons had he listed? Three? Piece of cake to list ninety-seven more. Charlotte was cultured. Sophisticated. And outside of her shopping expeditions, she often exhibited down-to-earth values.

"Damn pants," he muttered, giving them a tug. They were stuck on his hips. It was a miracle rock stars had sex lives...

With a forceful yank, he pulled at the zipper. It gave way with a loud metallic rip. Muttering an expletive, Russell peeled them down his body, kicked them aside and stepped into the shower.

The rush of water bounced off his hair. He should have forced a comb through the tangles first. Or maybe blasted a road down his part. "Wonderful," he sputtered. "One night with Liz the tattoo artist, and my hair will never be the same."

Or my heart.

The thought jolted him. *Those pants must have cut off circulation to my brain.* Squirting shampoo on his head, he mentally shifted gears. Charlotte's virtues. He had...ninety-four reasons to go. He'd treat it like a mantra. Keep repeating her virtues until he reached some kind of non-Harley, non-Liz nirvana.

Okay, Charlotte was well mannered. Well manicured. Well. Yes, definitely healthy. In the two years they'd been involved, she'd never had so much as a sniffle. Good genes to pass on to the kids.

Blinking back the soap, he massaged the froth into his helmet hairdo. And making love with her was lovely. Okay, somewhat predictable, but after several years that was inevitable. Just because something was predictable was no reason to trade it in for wild, hot, unbridled passion with a flame-haired vixen who could probably melt a twelve-year-old boy's braces just by looking at him.

"Good Lord. I'm back to the Liz fantasies." He twisted the water faucet. As a torrent of freezing water assaulted his body, he blinked fiercely and gasped for air. Sputtering, he repeated a line from Oscar Wilde. "'There is no sin except stupidity.'"

"MADAY PARTY? They're expecting you. This way, please," said the maître d' cooly. His voice had the measured cadence of a man accustomed to saying everything in the same range, same inflection. *There could be a raging fire*, Russell thought, *and this man would calmly say, "Inferno? This way, please."*

The maître d', crisply attired in a pin-striped suit, flicked his gaze up to Russell's hair before turning to lead the way.

I no longer have my own hair, Russell fumed. *It's become this entity that sits on my head. Two seats, please*, he thought, following the maître d' as he weaved expertly around the tables and diners. *One for me, one for my hair.*

The decor consisted of peach-hued walls, palm fronds and large white-glass balls. The latter hung from the ceiling like ominous hailstones. Glancing around, Russell wondered why an owner would request a "pastel South Pacific–hail" look for a French restaurant. Or maybe the decorator was into cross-culture-shock decors.

Only in L.A.

As they approached the Madays' table, the maître d' did a dancing half turn and gestured smoothly to the empty chair.

"Russ-ell!" called out Mrs. Maday, waving her fingers in a greeting. On her hands, diamonds sparkled like twinkling Christmas lights.

"Judith," responded Russell, taking her proffered hand and raising it to his lips. He might look like Eraserhead, but he could act like a gentleman. Like a saint, if need be. Tonight was kiss up to the family. Big time.

Lifting his head, he looked over the rest of the table.

Mr. Maday sat stiffly next to his wife. He looked as though someone had slipped him a lemon drop instead of a dinner mint. "Russell," he said with all the enthusiasm of one delivering a funeral oratory.

"Dona—Mr. Maday."

With a nod of his head, Mr. Maday indicated the woman on his right. "You remember Agnes, Mrs. Maday's cousin."

How could he forget the floating cloud. Russell plastered what he hoped passed as a warm smile on his face. "Of course. Agnes. Lovely to see you again."

Her gaze bounced up to his hair before landing back on his face. "Hullo. Nice to see you dressed so…nicely."

Mr. Maday grunted. "And her husband, Fred," he continued.

A small, bespectacled man nodded a greeting. "Russell. Pleased to see you again." Light glinted off his glasses as he looked up, then back down. His thin lips flinched a smile.

Russell glanced at Charlotte, who stared, aghast, at his hair.

He gave a polite cough. "I realize my…" he pointed at his head as though the word "hair" had suddenly escaped his vocabulary "—looks like a bad hat." He laughed, thinking the others might join in.

No one did. Not even a courtesy chortle.

Russell let his solitary laugh die down. He had a Zen moment of understanding the meaning of one hand clapping. It had to be similar to one man laughing.

"That horrid, angry student is the cause of all this," Mrs. Maday said, making an obvious move on Russell's behalf. She grasped his hand and smiled tremulously at her table companions. "Despite his unfortunate hairdo, our Russell has always exhibited good taste."

Hairdo?

Mrs. Maday continued to clutch Russell's hand as she addressed the group. "Of course he has good taste—he's marrying our daughter, isn't he?" She trilled a laugh that would have made Glenda the Good Witch proud. She turned and gave him a benevolent look. "We're so happy you'll be part of our family, dear."

He felt momentarily ashamed for every petty thing he had ever thought of Charlotte's mother. She was rising to the occasion, championing his cause. Being buried next to her for all eternity wasn't such a small price to pay for her kind words.

One down, four to go, Russell thought, easing a look at Charlotte.

She sat stiff backed, staring at some invisible spot on the tablecloth between the crystal vase and the silver salt shaker. Her platinum blond hair, pulled back in a sleek chignon, made her delicate features more prominent. Charlotte was blessed with a classical, cool beauty. Grace Kelly. Good.

She turned her icy blue eyes on him.

Grace Kelly. Bad.

She smiled. A smile he'd seen before. All movement, no emotion. She was an expert at hiding her true feelings. A lifetime in the upper crust had taught her well to never divulge what's below the surface.

"Please, Russell, have a seat," she said in a well-practiced tone that didn't reveal one iota of displeasure.

He pulled out the chair next to her, wondering how many courses he'd have to endure before the Ice Princess thawed.

After sitting down, he reached for her hand under the table and coiled his warm fingers around her lifeless ones. It was like holding hands with a mannequin. He wiggled his fingers inside her palm, which usually coaxed a smile.

Nothing.

Mr. Maday harrumphed, as though he knew what was going on. "Cocktails, everyone?" He wagged a finger at a waiter, who dutifully scurried over.

Murmurs of drink orders followed.

"Turkey, Russell?" asked Mr. Maday. A bit too loudly.

Russell waited a beat. Mr. Maday knew Russell always drank Wild Turkey on the rocks. He'd been drinking it ever since he started courting their daughter two-plus years ago. Abbreviating the familiarity was one thing. Abbreviating Wild Turkey to Turkey was another.

Why not just call me "jerk," he thought, but swallowed his retort and smiled pleasantly. "On the rocks. Thank you."

Appetizers proceeded smoothly. Not that anything tasted good to Russell. Here he was in one of the finest French restaurants in the city, and everything tasted like cardboard. With sauce.

Halfway though the main course, he groped under the table for Charlotte's hand again. As his fingers curled around hers, her pinkie twitched.

One small twitch for mankind. He was on his way home.

Mr. Maday was starting to call him "m'boy" again. Mrs. Maday wasn't fluttering her diamond-bedecked hands as much—a sign she was relaxing. Agnes was rambling on about some vacation she and her husband had recently taken to Greece. Fred, never saying a word, stared dolefully at his wife as though she were some creature to whom he must pay reluctant homage.

But Charlotte—Good, Grace Kelly, Thawing Ice-Princess Charlotte—was now squeezing Russell's hand under the table. Occasionally, she slid him a meaningful glance, her ice blue eyes now warmed to the color of a Caribbean azure sky.

He watched as she expertly speared a prawn out of its shell with the dexterity of a brain surgeon. Her slim, white hand lifted the forkful of food to her pink-frosted lips, nibbling at the food. Maybe later she'd nibble a little at him. A warmth curled up through his chest. Beautiful, classy, cultured Charlotte. A man couldn't ask for a better mate.

The world was right again. He envisioned the picket fence, the green lawn, the…God forbid…Shenkel-shaped latrine…but grotesque art was a minor sacrifice for the privilege of being married to the perfect Charlotte Maday.

Finishing the last bite of sauced cardboard, he grew aware that all conversation had ceased. Not only at their table, but throughout the room. Somewhere a crystal glass tinkled, the sound more deafening than a cannon boom.

Mrs. Maday raised one bejeweled hand to her throat. For a quirky moment, Russell wondered if a piece of her veal Cordon Bleu was wedged in her esophagus.

She blinked rapidly and stammered, "Th-the…"

He reached for his glass of water, ready to offer it to her.

Her blinking rate increased. "The angry student…" Her voice was barely above a whisper.

Russell froze midreach. The angry student meant…

Raven.

Icy cold washed over his skin. His gaze drifted across the room. All the diners' eyes were focused in the same direction.

Somewhere behind him.

Wonderful. Raven was probably hovering over his head, his meaty fists poised in a prestrangulation grip. Russell, trying to swallow a last morsel of sautéed spinach, looked up. His gaze met one of those oversize hailstones.

He craned his neck to look behind him.

Raven, dressed in his signature leather outfit—which looked a great deal more wrinkled—stood next to the hostess's podium, his beady black eyes scouring the restaurant.

From a nearby table, a woman's voice whispered, "Wasn't he the villain in that Sylvester Stallone movie? The psychopath who ate his victims?"

The spinach latched on to Russell's tonsils.

Raven raised his sausage-size finger and pointed at Russell. "There's the dude!" he bellowed.

Chairs squeaked as all bodies turned toward the Madays' table.

Raven, his chin jutting forward, stomped toward them. The maître d' waved frantically to one of the waiters. "Stop him," he mouthed. The waiter gave him an are-you-crazy look.

One table, celebrating someone's birthday, snapped a picture of Raven as he stormed past. He stopped, momentarily blinded.

"What the h—" he yelled.

A woman squealed, "I want his autograph."

Raven rubbed his eyes, then searched the room with his heat-seeking-missile gaze. Focusing again on the Madays, he lurched in their direction.

Charlotte gripped Russell's hand with a force reserved for crushing macadamias. "Darling," she said in a breathy voice that sounded oddly sexual to him. "Maybe we should invite the angry student to join us for a cocktail."

"A Pink Cadillac perhaps?" asked Russell in a choked voice. He wished the spinach would dissolve, drop, do something. It was beginning to feel like a hunk of mistletoe hanging off his tonsils. He made a mental note to hang only tinsel next Christmas.

If he lived that long.

And how the hell had Raven found him? A niggling suspicion about Drake's phone call crept into his consciousness.

The thought scattered as Raven shoved aside an empty chair at a neighboring table. Someone screamed. A waiter dropped a dish. The maître d', looking like one of those figures at Madame Tussaud's wax museum, stood transfixed at the podium.

I'll die at Chez Nous, Russell thought. A headline flashed through his mind. *English Professor Strangled At Chez*

Nous. His Last Words: "Please Pass The Sautéed Spinach."

Like a locomotive braking to a stop, Raven halted his massive frame behind Agnes. His chest heaving, he glared over her bouffant white hair at Russell.

I have a small arsenal of weapons between me and death, he thought. He glanced down at what was within reach. A spoon. A butter knife.

English Professor Strangled After Life-And-Death Battle With Butter Knife.

Death was ignoble.

He looked back up into Raven-the-Psychopath-Who-Ate-His-Victims's glowering face and smiled. Or tried to. With a mouth dry enough to cure tobacco, Russell's dehydrated lip caught on his right incisor.

Raven's Fu Manchu mustache stiffened. "You makin' a face at me, man?"

"Heavens, Russell, don't exacerbate the situation," chimed in Mrs. Maday.

Exacerbate? She never used that word. Probably looked it up before dinner tonight. Coughing slightly, Russell raised his hand to his mouth and tried to inconspicuously pull his errant lip back down. Mission accomplished, he asked, "Cocktail, Raven?", stealing Mr. Maday's peace-making line.

Raven crossed his ham-size arms over his chest and scowled, his bushy black eyebrows lowering like dark clouds over his eyes. The skull-and-crossbones earring dangled like a disembodied head on a noose. "Don't drink."

"Shirley Temple, perhaps?" Russell knew it was his death knell, but he felt reckless. If he was going to die, let them say he was entertaining to the end.

Unfortunately no one laughed. Mr. Maday shook his head as though it was the stupidest utterance he'd ever heard. Agnes, her eyes rolled up at Raven, whispered, "Was Shirley your girlfriend?"

On the word "girlfriend," Raven jerked as though he'd been poked with an electric cattle prod. His eyes, formerly beady, now enlarged into two black bullet holes. He un-folded his arms and put his hands on his hips. The move-ment stretched his T-shirt across his chest, causing the word "Mutha" to double in size.

Impressive move, Russell thought. Raven now looked like a referee for Satan. And the offending player, Russell, was going to be kicked out of the game of life any moment.

He started to say something—anything—but the spinach shifted, momentarily blocking his air passage. He thumped his chest and tried to gobble a breath.

"Don't try to outmacho this cretin," Charlotte admon-ished in a fierce undertone.

Frowning at Charlotte, Russell managed to inhale a thin stream of air. He could die suffocating and she'd think he was being overly masculine. But before he could gasp enough air to speak, Raven leaned over Agnes and slammed his hands down on the table. Her eyes widened as she slipped a glance at Raven's muscled, tattooed arms.

"You got her name on your tat." His voice sounded like the rumbling thunder of an oncoming storm.

"Heavens," Mrs. Maday squealed. "The language!"

Russell had a momentary urge to tell Mrs. Maday she was exacerbating the situation, but restrained himself. He was breathing again—that was all that counted.

"Let's take this outside," he suggested, lowering his voice to a Charles Bronson macho range. Which probably would have worked if the shifted mistletoe-spinach hadn't made him sound as if he had a sudden cold. He cleared his throat for another take. "Let's—"

"We ain't goin' nowhere, dude." Raven straightened and began walking around the table, his eyes never leaving Russell's face. "You and me, we got a showdown."

I'm in a bad cowboy movie. In a French restaurant. In-stead of a spaghetti Western, it's an escargot Western. Play it for what it's worth. Russell held his hands up in a con-ciliatory gesture. "Surely, Raven, force never solved any-thing—"

"Solves everything," Raven interrupted, getting dangerously close.

Charlotte dug her fingernails into Russell's arm. "Do something," she hissed.

"Like what? Stun him with my wit?"

Raven stopped beside Russell's chair. This close, Russell smelled damp leather. And cologne that smelled like disinfectant. Knowing Raven, maybe it was disinfectant. Something heavy landed on his shoulder. He slid his gaze over. Raven's chicken-size hand clutched the shoulder of his dinner jacket.

"You all think this dude is an upstarting citizen," began Raven, his baritone voice carrying across the room.

Upstarting? Russell winced. Worse than the misused word, Raven was revving up to do a speech at Chez Nous. And Russell had thought the pool party had been a disaster....

"Surely, Raven, we can discuss this in private—"

"Glad you brought the private part up," said Raven in a gruff aside, patting Russell's shoulder as though he were a long-lost friend. "Speaking of private..." he continued, his voice increasing in volume.

The birthday table snapped another picture.

Raven sidled behind Russell's chair. Both hands now rested on Russell's shoulders. "The time has come for this dude to face the music."

"Donald, do something," cried Mrs. Maday, her hands fluttering.

"I'll always love you," Charlotte simpered, easing her hand from Russell's.

In a rush of movement, Raven grabbed the lapels of Russell's jacket and yanked. With a god-awful ripping sound, the jacket fell away like meat off a bone. Next, Raven gripped Russell's shirt—

"Young man, this has gone far en—" Mr. Maday proclaimed, rising from his chair.

With a flourish, Raven tugged the shirt open.

Cool air assaulted Russell's bare chest. He closed his

eyes, not wanting to witness anything else. Ever. In this lifetime. Or the next.

For a long moment, there was a deafening silence. Not even the faintest chink of glass or whispered comment could be heard in the room.

"Liz?" Charlotte said with astonishment.

5

"LIZ?" Charlotte repeated. The word ended in an elongated buzzing sound. Z-z-z-z.

Like an angry bee, ready to sting, Russell thought.

Judith Maday frowned, causing her finely tweezed eyebrows to pinch together. "Liz Taylor?"

Russell cringed. Right. Liz Taylor. And her eight husbands' names were tattooed down his back—

"I asked you a question, Russell." Charlotte's voice had risen to a shrill pitch. Was that glass shattering?

"The lady asked you a question, dude," Raven echoed.

Lady? Chick or broad, maybe. But "lady"? Had Raven the Carnivore taken an etiquette class since he had last tried to kill Russell?

"Dude?" Raven prompted in an ominous tone. His meaty hands slid up Russell's shoulder, dangerously close to his neck. This was worse than between a rock and a hard place. This was between strangulation and brutal truth.

At the moment, strangulation seemed the better option.

"Russell?" Charlotte whimpered, dabbing at the corner of her eye with a tissue, careful not to mess her makeup. She had metamorphosed from bee to hurt heroine.

Russell looked longingly at the butter knife. Maybe if he angled the blade just right he could commit hara-kiri. But with his luck, he wouldn't be allowed a dignified death. Oh, no. The prissy maître d' would scoop up his lifeless form and take him into the kitchen where, in a matter of hours, he'd be a new menu item.

Loin of Russell béarnaise.

Russell chop grilled with olive oil and rosemary.

Or maybe something simple. Russell tartare. Prepared tableside.

He cleared his throat and looked around the table. Charlotte's family, their faces frozen in different expressions of horror and surprise, looked as if they were each posing for *The Scream* by Edvard Munch.

"I realize you're all wondering," he began, trying to sound casual, "what another woman's name is doing on my chest."

Silence.

"It's quite a silly story, actually. I mean, why would a grown man go to his bachelor party and end up with—" he laughed nervously "—a name *other* than his fiancée's on his chest? I mean, what kind of idiot would allow that to happen?"

Mrs. Maday had put on her reading glasses and was now staring at the tattoo, carefully mouthing the word "Liz."

"Keep goin'," Raven growled, intensifying his grip on Russell's shoulder. Shooting pains tore down Russell's back.

"And I'd love to explain it," he said quickly, wondering if shoulder bones broke easily. "You see, it was my bachelor party and I had had a few too many Wild Turkeys—my limit is *two*—" He flashed a meaningful see-I-am-conservative-despite-how-this-looks look to Mr. Maday, who unfortunately was eyeballing the tattoo along with Mrs. Maday and missed the glance.

"Anyway," Russell continued, "and even though I had made Drake promise there would be no mud wrestlers or strippers or women of that ilk, for some crazy reason—" he attempted to laugh again, but it came out like a strangled bark "—some wild, insane reason, I ended up on a Harley with this tattoo artist—"

"Women ain't elk," interrupted Raven. "You be disrespectful again and..." He reached over, grabbed a breadstick and snapped it in two.

"Could someone call off Igor..." Russell rolled his eyes upward, indicating Raven. "It would be much easier to explain this unfortunate incident if I didn't have to witness strength displays with food..."

"Ig—I mean, Raven—please sit down and join us," said Charlotte soothingly. Russell had never heard that tone of voice before. Probably learned it in some finishing-school class. How to Tame Wild Beasts While Dining. Or How to Speak So Your Fiancé Does Not End Up a Menu Item.

Mr. Maday motioned to a waiter, who approached the table but stopped at a safe distance.

"Bring an extra chair," ordered Mr. Maday.

"We've called the police," responded the waiter in a confidential tone.

Mr. Maday threw back his head and gave the waiter a withering look. "I asked for a chair, not an officer. Bring one and dismiss the other."

The waiter nodded briskly and scurried away. A chair materialized within moments.

"Mr. Raven, please sit down," requested Charlotte, patting the empty seat next to her. "And, Daddy, ask that nice waiter to bring Mr. Raven a menu." She smiled sweetly at her father and turned back to Russell. The smile slid off her face. "As you were saying?" The warmth in her voice had gone south. Winter had again set in.

Russell pulled his shirt closed. "Yes, uh, where was I—"

"On a Harley."

"Yes." He nodded too vigorously. "Yes, that's correct."

"With a tattoo artiste."

"Artist—"

"And you had too many Wild Turkeys." Charlotte was tapping her glass of champagne with her perfectly manicured pink-frosted nails. "How did you ever stay on a Harley after imbibing so much alcohol?"

"Luck?"

Charlotte gave him the same withering look her father had given the waiter.

"What's fooey grass?" asked Raven loudly, pointing at something on the menu.

"Foie gras, sir, is a pâté," a new waiter answered in a smooth-as-silk-I'll-pretend-you-have-class voice. His hooded eyes barely skirted the scene at the table before he returned his bored attention to Raven.

Must be on drugs, Russell thought. *Or immune to Hollywood hysteria.*

"Think I read about that in my magazine today," mumbled Raven, totally absorbed in reading the menu.

"And?" coaxed Charlotte, casting a searing look at Russell.

As he read the expression on her face, it kicked in that this was part of an ongoing conversation he had lost the thread of.

"And...?" he responded, trying to sound mature and caring, despite the fact he was dog-paddling madly in the middle of a themeless discussion.

"And gimme some of that duck with cherries," said Raven loudly to the waiter. "Never had that before."

Charlotte breathed in slowly, her perfect nostrils flaring oh so slightly. "Mr. Raven, please lower your voice. I'm trying to converse with my fiancé."

Raven quickly looked up, his skull-and-crossbones earring swinging. "Huh? Oh, yeah. Sorry." He lowered his voice and, stabbing his index finger at something on the menu, whispered to the waiter.

"Where did you go?" Charlotte demanded, staring Russell down.

This was better than "And." Now he had an idea what they were talking about. "To The Rose Tattoo."

"The play?" Agnes chimed in, leaning forward to hear every word.

"No," answered Russell, glancing at Agnes, "the...tattoo parlor."

"And you asked to be tattooed with the name Liz," surmised Charlotte.

He looked back at her. Her ill-contained rage wasn't as

daunting as she might have thought. Actually, she was flushed with a fiery passion he'd rarely seen in her before. For a fleeting moment, he wondered if he was the type of man she really needed.

"Did you ask for the name Liz?" she repeated.

"No."

Her lips formed a small O of confusion.

"Actually, I don't really remember being at the tattoo parlor. All those Wild Turkeys, you know. Can't recall getting the tattoo, much less why I'd request an aging movie star's name to be permanently inked on my body…"

Which was a lie. He did remember. But the memory had nothing to do with tattoos. It had to do with warm lips, silky hair and petal-soft skin.

He shifted in his seat, wishing the memories would rise upward and disappear into one of those oversize hailstones that dangled from the ceiling. His heat-swirling recollections were the real problem, not the tattoo.

But even as he wished it, the memory of that night clung to his senses. It was as though he had tumbled into a vat of passion and reemerged never to be the same. What had Racine said? "It is no longer a passion hidden in my heart: it is Venus herself fastened to her prey."

"Then how did you get home if you were that drunk?" Charlotte dropped her tissue. "You did go home that night, didn't you?"

Agnes eagerly leaned in closer.

Mrs. Maday's glasses slipped down her nose.

Mr. Maday and Raven crossed their arms over their chests.

Fred smirked.

"I took a taxi?" A giant pink-and-purple flying albatross could have swept him back to Santa Monica, for all he knew.

Charlotte lowered her gaze and sniffed. "Did you wake up in your own bed, Russell?"

Raven snapped another breadstick in two.

"Of course, Char darling. I woke up with a ferocious

hangover in my very own bed. You called—remember?—and woke me up. I may be stupid, but I'm not dumb." He wasn't sure what that meant, but decided to blunder on, anyway. "I love you, Char. Please forgive my senseless, inconsiderate act. Let's not let a moment of foolishness destroy our happiness."

Agnes picked up her napkin and dabbed at her eyes. "This is better than *Dr. Zhivago.*"

Mrs. Maday blinked and removed her glasses. "You poor dear man. One mistake shouldn't cost you a lifetime of happiness."

Mr. Maday grunted and unfolded his arms.

Fred snorted.

A small smile teased Charlotte's lips. "Silly of me to ask where you slept. Sorry, darling."

Russell reached over and touched her fingertips. He was on a roll. The family was on his side.

He glanced at Fred's ill-disguised sneer.

Well, *most* of the family was on his side.

"Just one more question," continued Charlotte, tracing an imaginary pattern on the linen tablecloth. "You didn't do it because of that girl, right?"

"What girl?"

"That…that motorcycle heathen in the leather outfit that leaves nothing to the imagination."

"Oh. *That* girl." He made an exaggerated motion of denial. "Even if I was single, I wouldn't fall for a woman like that—"

Raven reached for another breadstick.

"Please, Raven. Break something else, okay?" Russell's nerves were shot. The past few days had been a roller coaster of emotions. He'd snap if one more breadstick did.

"It was a horrendous comedy of errors," Russell announced to the family. "I'm doing my best to have this thing removed—"

"By the wedding," added Charlotte.

"That's less than a week—"

"I will not marry a man who sports another woman's

name—even if she is in her sixties and no longer has an acting career.''

"Liz don't act," chimed in Raven. His forehead compressed into ridges of consternation as he stared, perplexed, at Charlotte. "You sure she's that old?" The ridges deepened until his forehead looked like the bars of a musical score.

Frightening how a deep thought changes some faces, Russell thought.

Enough reflection on Raven's facial contortions. Russell had to backpedal quickly. Change the course of this conversation before the real identity of Liz became known.

Charlotte shifted to face Raven. "Haven't you seen her in those perfume commercials? Surely she's in her—"

"Liz is immortal," Russell loudly interrupted. "As behooves any star of her stature."

Raven's forehead compressed further. "Bee-hooves?"

Russell swept his hand through the air in a grandiose don't-interrupt-me gesture. "But what really matters, Char, is that we move beyond this—" he began buttoning his shirt''—this...nonsense. I'll do everything within my power to have it removed by Saturday. And if I can't—''

Her blue eyes flashed ice. "No can'ts—"

"We'll cover it with a bandage—"

"I said, no can'ts—"

"You can call me Dick?"

Fred snorted again.

Russell cut him a look. "As in Dick and Liz."

"Of course," said Fred under his breath, suddenly interested in something on the ceiling.

"I don't want to call you Dick," said Charlotte with a pout. "I want to call you Russell on my wedding night. And I want no other woman's name coming between us." Her voice had softened. She reached over and stroked Russell's hand. "When I'm Mrs. Harrington, I want only you and me in our wedding bed. It will be the beginning of our life together. A life filled with happy days. And, if we're blessed, happy little feet—"

A loud sniff cut off the rest of her sentence.

Everyone at the table turned to look at Raven.

He swiped at his eyes with the back of his hand. "That's all I ever wanted, too."

He grabbed a linen napkin and blew his nose with it. The sound reverberated through the room. "What's wrong with the world today?" he said in a choked voice. "Why can't a dude love his woman, marry her and live happily ever after?" He stuffed the linen napkin in his back pocket. "And let her dance with her happy little feet if that's what she wants..."

Smiling, Charlotte reached over with her other hand and grabbed Raven's. Holding both Russell's and Raven's hands, she looked around the table, her eyes shimmering with tears. "And he can." Her gaze landed back on Russell. "As soon as the tattoo is removed." She smiled, her chin quivering with what Russell presumed to be uncontained joy.

Or ill-disguised ultimatum.

He preferred the fiery passionate look.

Carrying a silver-domed plate, the waiter stopped short at the table. His eyes barely flickered at the sight of Charlotte Maday, society-page regular, holding hands with a leather-clad cretin and a suit-shrouded gentleman.

"Duck with cherries," he announced drolly.

"YOU ATE WHAT?" Liz said as she closed the door to The Rose Tattoo and flipped the sign to Closed. It had been a late evening of tattooing. She was ready to call it a night. Especially because tomorrow was to be a day of heavy-duty wedding-dress shopping with Auntie. Liz couldn't wait to ride home, sink into a hot bath and down a bowl of green chili.

"Duck with berries?" she asked, turning around.

Raven sat sprawled across the wing chair, his crinkled leather pants riding up a good two inches above his ankles. "With cherries," he answered seriously. "And for dessert I had a cream bowl."

She blinked. "Cream bowl?"

Raven leaned forward, his oversize hands miming something small and round. "Had a thin burnt-sugar crust on the top. Crunchy and sweet. Didn't see that recipe in any of them mags you bought me, though."

Liz flicked a switch. The outside red neon light snapped off. Late-night Hollywood Boulevard traffic hummed past the window. A kid whizzed by on a skateboard, his head dipping to unheard music.

"You mean ice-cream bowl?" She pulled down the blinds over the front window.

"Cream bowl. They spelled it wrong on the menu, but I didn't say nuthin'. Want me to help clean up?"

She glanced over her shoulder. Raven looked like a schoolboy hanging around after class, wanting to be teacher's pet. An oversize, leather-clad, tattooed schoolboy. Not too many people knew that the guy had a heart of gold. She had a soft spot for him—just not the kind of soft spot he had in mind.

"I finished putting away the paint tubes. Thanks, anyway." She sighed heavily, rubbing a spot on her neck. "That last guy took forever. Wanted a map of the United States on his chest. Took his *entire* chest. I was going to skip Alaska and Hawaii, but he insisted I put them on his shoulder and elbow."

"Must be a world traveler."

"Well, a U.S. traveler, anyway." She picked up a few magazines and stacked them on a side table. "Or maybe he's a geography teacher."

As soon as she said it, she wished the words back. Reminded her of another teacher. An English professor. And the tattoo he had wanted late one night...

She straightened and changed the subject. "Since when did Meat Me on Fairfax start serving such gourmet-sounding dishes?" Meat Me on Fairfax was Raven's nightly dinner hangout. It served everything from hot dogs to meat loaf to spareribs. The decor consisted of cardboard cows painted with globs of black and white. The dive was a vegetarian's nightmare. In fact, the kind of food that gave most people nightmares, although Raven swore he slept like a baby after eating there.

"Wasn't at Meat Me on Fairfax. Dined with some folks elsewhere."

"Dined?" This was a new word for Raven. "Chowed down," maybe. "Grabbed some grub," definitely. But "dined"? She rearranged some plastic flowers on the bookshelf, waiting for further explanation. When none was given, she glanced back at Raven.

"You *dined* with some folks?"

Raven was staring intently at the faux Tiffany lamp on the table next to him. The reds, blues and yellows splashed on his face, but didn't disguise a tell-tale hint of red creeping up his neck.

"Raven, you're blushing," she said, surprised. "Are you...dating someone?"

He avoided her gaze.

She stared at him in wonderment. Raven, dating? Which wouldn't be a bad thing. If Raven had a girlfriend, he wouldn't take his marriage to Liz that seriously. She tugged on a strand of her hair. But would a girlfriend understand that Raven had to marry someone else as a temporary measure?

"Nah, I'm not dating." His face flushed a deeper crimson as he slid her a sideways glance.

Okay, so there was no girlfriend. But she'd seen this look before and it wasn't good. The last time Raven had a face the color of a persimmon was when—after bouncing a drunk customer from her parlor—he slammed the front door so hard that the front plate-glass window shattered. Cost her a week's income to replace it.

"Spill," she insisted.

He lowered his eyes to the floor. "You're gonna be pi—uh, mad."

"Is it going to cost me more than the plate-glass window?"

He shook his head. The ponytail flicked back and forth.

"Then why should I be mad?"

"Because..." He lifted his eyes and cast her a woebe-gone look reminiscent of a basset hound. His gaze shifted to something against the far wall, next to the couch.

She followed Raven's glance. "Because of—" her eyes landed on the portrait of her dad hanging on the wall "—my dad?"

"Lower."

She looked down at the small metal table she'd bought at a garage sale years ago. "The table?"

"Higher."

She expelled a sigh. "Raven, there's nothing between the table and the picture except the wall and you haven't put your fist through that particular one lately, so what is there for me to be mad about?" He was growing more sensitive daily. Maybe she shouldn't have bought him all those women's magazines.

He swung his size-thirteen foot back and forth. "What's on the table?"

"The message machine." She frowned. "Is it broken?"

He expelled a weighty sigh. "I listened to your messages."

She was prepared to hear about something he had broken, not listened to. The confession took her by surprise. "When?"

"You was with Auntie at the grocery store. I got bored lying in bed with nuthin' on, so I put on my wet outfit." He lifted his foot. The pant leg hit him several inches above the ankle. "They don't fit the same, by the way. That pool party ruined my best suit. Anyways, thought I'd head down here and help you open up. You know, like I do..." His voice trailed off.

True. He often helped her around the shop. She'd entrusted him with keys to the place several years ago. But what was it with the message machine? "You've listened to my work messages before," she prompted.

He turned his head toward her. His bushy eyebrows shot up in a look of anguished expectation.

Yep, he definitely expected her to get mad. Very mad.

"Who called?" she asked cautiously.

He cleared his throat. "Some dude. Drake somethin'. He, uh, said that Russell would give back them leather pants tomorrow because he, uh, was at dinner with his family..."

"Russell?" she said quickly. Her heart stuttered a beat. A rush of memories heated her insides. Russell pressed against her as they sped down Hollywood Boulevard. The heat of his lips as they grazed hers. The way her insides caved in when he said her name...

"Liz?" asked Raven.

She pulled out of her reverie and looked into Raven's basset-hound gaze. Foggily, the reason for their conversation floated to the top of her consciousness. The phone machine. Messages.

"It's okay that you listened, Raven. I trust you with my business."

She thought her words would calm him, but his woebegone look intensified. Poor guy. His jealousy over Russell had caused all heck to break loose. He was probably thinking that anything he did in conjunction with Russell would have negative implications. Even listening to one little message about Russell.

Russell.

She smiled as his name turned over in her thoughts. The name suited his professor personality. Not too brusque. But soothing. Sensual. Saying his name made her tongue trip softly against the roof of the mouth. "Russ-ell," she said under her breath.

"What 'bout him?" asked Raven.

"I'm...just thinking about that message..."

She turned away so he wouldn't see the smile creeping across her face. Now it was her turn to blush. Her turn to feel like a schoolgirl. It had been years since she'd felt this giddy over a single phone call.

Tomorrow.

Russell would be here tomorrow. She'd leave a message

on her machine that she'd be back around five. Didn't want to miss him. No, sir.

She breathed in deeply, knowing it wouldn't calm her thoughts. What to wear, what to wear. Her red dress with the cowboy boots? No. One blush and she'd look like a stop sign. Maybe the turquoise jeans outfit. She held up a hand and scrutinized her fingers. Get a manicure? She mimed reaching for the leather pants as Russell handed them to her. Yes, definitely a manicure. She wanted to look perfect when she reached for those pants. Who knew? Maybe he'd ask her out for a drink after work or...

A thought slammed through her pants-encounter fantasy. Warning bells clanged in her head.

She dropped her hand and slowly turned to Raven. "You said you...dined with some folks?"

He nodded slowly.

"What folks?"

"Russell's folks?"

"Are you asking or telling?"

He straightened and lowered his voice. "Russell's folks." His oversize feet were now swinging across the floor in record time.

She sank into a nearby chair. "Duck with cherries. Cream bowl." She groaned and dropped her head into her hands. "Crème brûlée."

"Yeah, that's how the waiter pronounced it."

She didn't want to look up. She wanted to remain forever with her head in her hands, not seeing anything but the small black cave of her palms. A gulp escaped her lips, part hysteria, part breath.

"You okay, Liz?"

"I'll never be okay again," she mumbled into her hands.

"What? Can't hear ya."

She looked up. "I'll never be—oh, never mind." She crossed her arms under her breasts and stared at Raven. "Tell me the worst. Skip the appetizers and chitchat. I want to know exactly what you did that will haunt me for the rest of my life."

Raven stopped swinging his feet and stretched his legs forward. Hairy ankles protruded from his shortened pants. "Russell's shirt was opened."

"What's that supposed to mean? Did someone open his present by mistake?"

"Uh, it means..." He paused, then rushed through the rest of the sentence. "I opened his shirt."

She waited a beat. "While it was on him?"

"Yeah."

A moment of silence extended into a small eternity. The only sound was the hum of traffic from Hollywood Boulevard.

"Everyone saw the tat?" she said slowly, enunciating each word.

"Yeah."

"Everyone?"

He nodded, his brow creasing into a thick stack of folds. "Charlotte, her parents...?"

"Some other people, too. Didn't catch their names. And of course everyone else in the restaurant."

Charlotte fidgeted with the fringe on her jacket. "His life is ruined," she said quietly.

Raven jumped to his feet, his huge hands pumping the air as though he didn't know what to do with them. "Don't fret, Liz. The professor and Char—I mean, Charlotte—talked it through and they're stayin' together. You shoulda been there. They told each other how much they loved each other and how this wouldn't stand between them..." He sniffed loudly. "It was heart-jerkin', I tell ya."

She looked at Raven swiping at his eyes. That was it, no more magazines.

And no more Russell.

"They made up, you mean?" *They told each other how much they loved each other.* Her heart contracted a little.

"Yeah." He smiled so widely that his silver bicuspid flashed.

She wanted to be happy. After all, she didn't want his

life ruined. Didn't want *anyone's* life ruined, including Charlotte's.

Even so, a growing ache throbbed within Liz. Okay, so she knew she was turned on by the guy. But in that instant she also realized how deeply Russell had affected her.

Seemed silly, something that brief affecting her so. After all, she had survived the death of her dad, managed the family tattoo shop all by herself, struggled to build her own business. It hadn't been easy, but as her dad had always said, she had a soul of iron.

She swallowed hard. *But even a soul of iron can't protect a broken heart.*

"You okay, Liz?"

Raven's voice penetrated her cocoon of hurt. "Fine. I'm fine," she murmured.

She squared her shoulders. And she would be fine. Okay, so a momentary fling had hit her with the impact of a full-blown love affair. Whoever said life was simple? She was a survivor—she'd survive this. One thing was for sure: the next time some poetry-spouting ivory-tower type stumbled into her life, she'd show him the exit, pronto. No hanging out listening to sweet words, sharing even sweeter kisses.

All her growing-up years, her dad had warned her of the bad-boy types. She laughed to herself. He should have warned her of the witty, intellectual types, as well.

Wit and brains. Lethal combo. Never again.

She pasted a smile on her face. "Fine," she repeated. "But let's you and me make a pact. No more hunting down the professor, okay?"

Raven's eyes moistened. "Deal."

"He has his own wedding coming up—and we have ours. No reason for you to be jealous of anyone."

"Our wedding," Raven repeated. He grinned and clasped his hands together. "I'll make you proud of me, Liz."

Her smile turned genuine. Maybe Russell was marrying for love, but she wasn't doing so badly herself. She'd be marrying her best buddy, a man with a heart as big as his feet.

"You already make me proud, Raven."

6

THE DAILY 6:00 p.m. cocktail hour at the Madays was as scrupulously planned and attended as High Mass at the Vatican.

Or so Russell had long ago come to believe. Around four, Wendel began laying out the crystal glasses, silver ice bucket and an array of beverages in preparation for the service.

By five, fresh flowers had arrived, which one of the housekeepers meticulously arranged around the sitting room and altarlike marble table that ran along one wall. During winter, a cozy fire burned gaily in the fireplace. During summer, the windows opened out on the lush front lawns.

By six, the Madays and guests assembled for an hour of communion with one another to the background of soft classical music and tinkling ice cubes. An unspoken rule was semiformal attire, which developed over the years out of respect for the daily ritual.

"The usual, sir?" Wendel asked, standing quietly at Russell's elbow.

Russell glanced at the antique cherrywood clock on the mantel. Six o'clock sharp. Ever punctual, that Wendel. The Swiss probably set time by his habits.

"We've discussed this 'sir' thing before," said Russell in a low voice, running a finger along the inside of his collar. He'd worn a tie tonight, the gray silk one Mrs. Maday bought for his last birthday. He viewed it as a symbolic goodwill gesture, especially needed after the near fiasco at Chez Nous.

He also needed another suit, as he was down to his last one. Raven had ripped the sleeve off the one he'd worn last night. At least it was the sleeve and not Russell's neck.

Thank God for small favors.

Across the room, Mr. Maday was coddling his Scotch while pontificating on the latest trends in the stock market to Fred. Agnes and Mrs. Maday were seated on the couch, fiddling with a gold-wrapped package. Their heads bobbed in conversation.

"Yes, we have discussed it, sir," Wendel responded.

Russell leveled him a dead-on stare. "You didn't call me 'sir' before the engagement. Now you treat me as though I'm next in line to the throne."

"Only because Prince Charles blew his opportunity."

Even as he chuckled, Russell felt a twinge of guilt. "Do you share this biting wit with the Madays?"

"Only when they're not listening."

"Which means most of the time." Russell stuck his hands into his trouser pockets and rocked back on his heels. He had always felt more comfortable around Wendel than any of Char's family. "Let's let our hair down soon and enjoy a drink together. What do you say?"

"Certainly." Wendel flicked his eyes up, then back down. "For now, Wild Turkey, sir?"

Russell narrowed his gaze. "Okay, so my hair is almost back to normal. You're dying to know what happened, right?"

"I'm breathless with anticipation."

Russell did a double take before continuing. "It stood on end for several days because I decided to ride around on the back of a Harley in the wee hours of the morning after one too many Wild Turkeys." He cocked one eyebrow. "Let this be a warning to you, my good man. If you ever overimbibe, refuse to get into—or sit astride—a vehicle that doesn't have a roof."

"Warning taken, sir."

Russell winced. "Yes, Wild Turkey. Thank you."

Wendel exited toward the bar.

Charlotte glided into the room, her svelte figure neatly encased in a gossamer gown that would have made Aphrodite jealous. Her blond hair fell loosely about her face, framing her finely chiseled features in a golden, frothy haze. She stopped behind the couch and began talking animatedly with Agnes and her mother.

Russell barely felt the drink Wendel put into his hand. All he could think was that Charlotte Maday was the most beautiful creature God had ever created. Like an exquisite statue come to life. And he, Russell Harrington, a mild-mannered professor of English literature, was the lucky man to have won this goddess's heart.

He breathed in deeply and caught a whiff of her flowery perfume. ''Aphrodite, eat your heart out,'' he said under his breath.

He took a sip of bourbon, savoring its familiar, pleasant sting. He had almost blown it with Charlotte. Almost thrown it all away because of one impassioned evening with a flame-haired temptress. What had Charlotte called her? He closed his eyes, recalling her words. *''Motorcycle heathen in the leather outfit that leaves nothing to the imagination.''*

Whoa. She had that last part right. Liz and those second-skin leather outfits could make a dead man come to life.

He took another sip, rolling the pungent liquid in his mouth. Its burn reminded him of Liz's kisses. Ardent, hot.

''Russell, why are you standing there with your eyes closed?''

Charlotte's voice yanked him out of the fantasy.

He popped open his eyes.

A sickening ripple of déjà vu rinsed over him. Just like last night at Chez Nous. Everyone in the room was staring at him. At least this time Raven wasn't standing behind him, baring Russell's chest for all the world to see.

''Just contemplating…your beauty,'' he lied.

Charlotte dipped her head to the side and eyed him curiously. ''With your eyes closed?''

''Imagining your beauty on our wedding day.'' He raised

his glass. "Let's toast Charlotte's beauty on our wedding day. Any day, for that matter. Today, even. This very moment." He had to get his act together. Cool it with the Liz fantasies. Tonight he'd take another cold shower and itemize Charlotte's qualities all over again. Starting at one hundred.

Murmurs of praise were followed by everyone raising their glasses to Charlotte.

Smiling coyly, she crooked her finger at Russell. "Darling, come tell Mommy where we'll be honeymooning."

He took another sip to steel himself, making a mental note that his children would never call Charlotte and him "Mommy" and "Daddy."

He crossed to the couch and sidled next to Charlotte. They had agreed that the honeymoon was his gift to her, which meant a trip *he* could afford. Which also meant he had to find the right words to assure the Madays he was giving their daughter the very best, despite the fact most garbage collectors had higher salaries than English professors.

"We're planning a short trip to the wine country," he began.

Agnes jumped a little, which shook the couch. "Italy? How romantic."

Russell attempted a pleasant smile. "No, actually—"

"France? Bordeaux country?" asked Mrs. Maday.

He looked down at her smiling, remarkably unlined face. She thought everyone could afford trips to France, no doubt. If he ever showed her his paycheck stub, she'd probably think it was a receipt for dinner.

He gripped his glass tighter. "No, we're…"

Mr. Maday and Fred had sauntered over, joining the couch crowd. The room suddenly felt claustrophobic. Russell cleared his throat. "We're heading up to Valley of the Moon."

They all stared at him as though he had said they'd be flying to the moon. "Valley of the Moon," he repeated. "Jack London country."

"Jack who?" Agnes said.

"A writer," Russell explained. "Long dead. Not important." He took another sip. A warm breeze wafted through the opened window, bringing a small relief to the stuffy atmosphere.

Charlotte wound her arm through his. "We're going to Northern California's wine country where we'll wine and dine and—"

"Sounds fine," cut in Mr. Maday, "we don't need particulars."

Charlotte giggled. "Oh, Daddy. I'll always be your little girl."

Daddy. An image flashed in Russell's mind. He and Char, in their sixties, sitting in this same room at six o'clock sharp. Char, her hair silvered, her back slightly bent, talking to Daddy and Mommy.

Russell motioned to Wendel that he needed a refill.

Mr. Maday grunted. "Northern California. Nice."

Fred smirked.

Mrs. Maday waved her diamond-sprinkled hand at the group. "I think it sounds divine. Valley of the Swoon. How positively romantic."

Russell started to correct her when Agnes erupted in a high-pitched squeal.

"Oh, Judith, let's share our surprise with Charlotte now," she said, wriggling in anticipation. The couch shimmied with her movements.

"Yes, let's," oozed Mrs. Maday, reaching for the gold box on the table. "Charlotte, baby, Agnes and I wanted you to wear this on your wedding day. You know, 'something borrowed, something blue'—well, this is your 'something borrowed.' Except that we want you to keep it."

"Mommy, didn't you bring me up to return things I borrowed?" Charlotte teased as she eagerly opened the package and extracted what Russell at first thought was a string of tinsel.

"Your tennis bracelet! Oh, Mommy!" Charlotte lifted it

slightly higher for the rest to see. It sparked small blasts of light, just like the diamonds on Mrs. Maday's hands.

"Daddy, can you fasten the clasp?" asked Charlotte, traipsing over to her father. After he finished, she again held up the bracelet for everyone to admire.

"This is a memorable evening," enthused Agnes, clapping her hands together. "Let's do something special to celebrate."

"Not dinner," Mr. Maday said sharply, casting a glance at Russell.

"Perhaps the theater?" said Mrs. Maday quickly.

"Wonderful idea," concurred Charlotte. "Wendel, please bring us a newspaper. You know which section." He disappeared into the other room. "After last night's drama, let's see something light. A romantic comedy," Charlotte said with a giggle, twisting her wrist this way and that as she eyed the bracelet.

Her sudden humor sent cold shivers down Russell's spine. Although he was glad she was putting last night behind her, he was certain that for many years it would rank in his top-ten all-time life nightmares. He comforted himself with another sip of bourbon.

Wendel reappeared with a folded newspaper and handed it to Charlotte. She thanked him and crossed the room to a side table, where she laid the paper out.

"Northern California," continued Mr. Maday, who'd obviously been mulling over their honeymoon location. "For a first honeymoon. But someday, after your literary criticism career takes off, a European honeymoon."

Russell ran his finger along the inside of his collar again. The tie was beginning to feel like a noose. This family seemed to think he would be the next William Safire—or some such grammatical, book-writing, moneymaking monument. Whatever dreams he might have had for himself seemed unimportant. Maybe they were. After all, dreams inevitably led to failure.

But before he could stammer a safe, noncommittal reply, Charlotte shrieked.

Everyone froze.

"You...you..." Charlotte's frothy hairdo looked as though it had been zapped with an electrical current. Hunched over the paper, she was staring at Russell with a look that seemed uncomfortably familiar.

Because it was the same look she'd given him last night during the tattoo unveiling.

He quickly looked down.

No, his shirt was buttoned. And his jacket was buttoned over the shirt.

He jerked his head back up and met her gaze. Was she having a tattoo flashback?

"You!" she repeated, pointing her pink fingernail at him. The diamond bracelet dangled from her wrist like a ring of fire. "You...you..."

"Me?" Russell answered, too stunned to think of anything else to say. Even if he could have, he didn't have the breath to say it. The damn tie was cutting off all flow of air.

Wendel handed him a fresh drink. Russell clutched it with the desperation of a man grasping a life preserver.

Charlotte stabbed her frosty pink fingernail at the paper, not taking her accusing gaze off Russell. "How could you?" she whined, stomping her foot. Which, on the three-inch-thick carpeting, sounded more like a foomp than a stomp. "Oh, Mommy," she cried, opening her slim arms toward her mother on the couch.

Mrs. Maday went into immediate Mommy mode and was at Charlotte's side within seconds. "Baby, what's the matter?"

Agnes was on the edge of her seat. Russell swore the couch was tipping slightly. That or the bourbon was taking effect. He debated whether to apologize—although he still didn't have the foggiest what egregious crime he had committed.

"Mommy," Charlotte wailed again, dropping her head on her mother's shoulder.

Mrs. Maday coiled her arms around her daughter.

"There, there, now, little pumpkin. What did you see in that paper that's so bad?"

Against all logic, Russell prayed it was merely a missed sale at Neiman's.

Mrs. Maday looked at where Charlotte was pointing in the paper.

"Donald," she breathed, pawing her hand in the air for her husband.

Mr. Maday, jolted into action, stormed over to his wife and daughter. After glancing at the paper, he embraced his spouse and child in a protective hold while lowering a penetrating gaze at Russell.

After a moment's uncomfortable silence, Russell cleared his throat. "Did someone die?"

"Not yet," said Mr. Maday thickly.

Russell took another sip. This was like watching a bad rerun of "Father Knows Best." Only he wasn't watching; he had stepped into the damn TV set.

Fred moved in, peeked over Mrs. Maday's shoulder at the paper and smirked.

The guy probably visits funeral homes for a laugh. "Uh, could someone tell me what the problem is?" asked Russell.

Agnes waddled over to the family gathering and stuck her nose close to the paper. "Darn. Wish I'd brought my glasses. What are we looking at?"

Mr. Maday puffed out his chest and pulled his daughter and wife closer. Charlotte was at the loud sniffling phase. Full-blown crying would be next.

Russell pulled his drink closer. Ever since the fateful evening of his bachelor party, his life had been on a rapid spiral downward. If he survived this latest setback, he'd personally lobby for a law to make bachelor parties illegal.

"Russell," said Mr. Maday, sounding ominously like Charlton Heston in *The Ten Commandments.* "Come here and explain this."

He crossed the room to the Maday newspaper reunion. His legs felt wooden, heavy. As though he were walking to the guillotine. He had an urge to ask for a last cigarette, except he didn't smoke.

When he reached the family gathering, they stepped back in unison, like some sort of macabre chorus line. He pretended not to notice their unsociable behavior as he leaned over and searched the newsprint and pictures.

A shoe ad. A restaurant opening.

A picture.

He closed his eyes. *Please, God, let this be a bad dream and not reality.*

He opened his eyes. Yes, it was *the* picture.

Russell, bare chested with a head of hair that looked as though he were the bride of Frankenstein, kissing a woman. Not just any woman. No, the motorcycle heathen in the leather outfit that leaves nothing to the imagination.

The picture Auntie took of him and Liz. An *engagement* picture.

Russell stared at the newspaper longer than he needed. Partly out of shock. Partly out of fear. When he raised his head and met the Maday family's ensemble stare, he would have to have something to say. Something intelligent. Reasonable. Plausible.

He straightened and cleared his throat. "Would you believe my pants were soaked after that tumble in the pool and that woman—" he jabbed his thumb toward the paper as though they might have no idea who "that woman" might be "—found me a pair of too-small leather pants from her horror-writer neighbor and her auntie showed up and I pretended I was her fiancé because it was either that or be killed or possibly eaten alive by Raven the Carnivore and I had no idea the picture would ever ever go into the newspaper so help me God."

He paused to inhale a lungful of stale air.

Charlotte, her mascara dribbling down her face, raised her head from her father's shoulder. "You pretended to be engaged to that...that...motorcycle heathen?"

"Only out of survival instinct, I assure you."

"Young man, I think you should leave," commanded Mr. Maday.

"Char, I can explain—"

"You've done enough explaining," Mr. Maday warned.

Russell continued heedlessly. "This looks far worse than what really happened."

Everyone turned slightly and looked at the picture.

"You're kissing her!" Charlotte howled. She turned away and buried her face in her father's chest. "What could be worse?"

"Char," Russell began. But Mr. Maday's I'll-kill-you-for-hurting-my-little-girl look momentarily stopped him.

He decided to focus on the group as a whole. One more look into Mr. Maday's eyes might turn Russell into stone. "Everyone," he said, starting over, "I apologize for this terrible misunderstanding. I'll clear this matter up. First, I'll demand a formal apology from the newspaper. And second…"

He set his drink down on a coffee table. "Second, I'll put an end to this nonsense once and for all."

He pivoted on his heel and headed for the front door. He knew what he'd do. Head straight to The Rose Tattoo and have a word or two with Ms Motorcycle Heathen about Photog Auntie. These little escapades were ruining his wedding, his future, his life.

He stopped in front of the oversize front door and reached for the gargantuan brass doorknob. Halting midreach, he stared at first the knob, then the door. After all this time, a thought hit him. What did the Madays have? A *Gulliver's Travels* complex?

It made him feel small. Insignificant.

Or had he always felt that way with the Madays?

He jerked the door open and stepped outside. But before he shut it behind him, he heard Agnes say to the group, "I guess the theater is out of the question?"

THE DAILY 6:00 p.m. rush hour on the 101 was as chaotic and crowded as last call at Barney's, the bar on Santa Monica Boulevard where Liz used to be a regular.

Used to. One more late night of partying, dancing and stale pickup lines and she'd have collapsed from overpartyitis. Nearly a year ago it finally dawned on her that the L.A. bar scene was nothing but a revolving door of cardboard cutouts. Everyone either waited on tables or sold retail. During their off-hours they auditioned for their big showbiz break. Night after night she found herself nodding and listening to the same conversation. Only the faces changed.

These days, instead of sitting on a bar stool after work, she'd sit astride her Harley and roar up Highway 1. And instead of seeking company with wanna-be movie stars, she listened to the pounding of the distant surf and wrote sonnets. Later, at her Hollywood apartment, she would heat up a dinner of green chili before curling up with a good book.

Except for the other night. Feeling a little lonely, she had dropped by Satiricon for a relaxing glass of wine. And instead of sitting next to some pretty boy who aspired to star in a soap, she sat next to a charming man who aspired to crawl out of the academic niche that life had carved for him.

Russell.

All day she'd spent trudging the shopping malls with Auntie, but her mind had been on Russell. Maybe this evening he'd drop by The Rose Tattoo to return her neighbor's pants. Just in case, she'd worn her turquoise jeans outfit. It fitted her snugly, outlining some of her better qualities. Okay, she wanted to appeal to the guy. Was that a crime?

Yes, if the guy was set to marry somebody else in less than a week.

She cranked down the passenger window of Auntie's car. Hot air and gas fumes blasted through the open window. Sunlight reflected off another car's chrome bumper and zapped her in the eyes like a searing laser.

That's what she needed. Laser brain surgery to remove her thoughts, her memories, of Russell. A mind tuck. Surely such a thing could be done in L.A., where every type of surgery known to stardom was available.

"Sweetie," said Auntie, interrupting Liz's surgical fantasies.

"Yes?" She looked over at Auntie's powdered face. Auntie had probably never spent a day in the sun. Her pale cheeks matched the pallor of her petite hands, which gripped the steering wheel of her decade-old Audi.

Sitting here reminded Liz of being a little girl during one of Auntie's visits. She'd show up at the carnival, as prim and neat as she looked today, carrying a brand-new book as a gift for her "special niece." They'd spend long afternoons sitting side by side, absorbed in a story about Oz or Narnia or some other magical place, taking turns reading different passages aloud.

"Ever hear of 'something old, something new, something borrowed, something blue'? Well, we got you something new," Auntie said, her sparkling eyes focused on the Cadillac in front of her. "But you still need something borrowed, blue and old."

Liz dragged her hand through her hair. In the lane next to her, loud rap music blared out of a cherry red Impala with the words Lover Boy stenciled along the side of the car. Lover Boy, probably no older than sixteen, sat low in the driver's seat, rolling a toothpick between his full lips. He caught Liz staring at him and grinned lasciviously. The toothpick stuck straight at her like a probe.

He should rename his car Toothpick Boy, Liz thought.

"Did you hear me, sweetie?" Auntie asked, turning her head slightly.

Liz looked back. "We need something loaned and blue."

"Not loaned. *Borrowed.* Ever hear of that saying? We also need something blue and something old."

Liz twisted a strand of hair around her finger. "What about Raven's old Volkswagen?" She smiled at the resurrected memory. God forbid anyone should learn that Raven, the King of Biceps, used to work as a florist's apprentice in Etiwanda and had driven a baby blue VW.

Auntie's brow creased in fine lines of consternation. "Old Volkswagen?"

"It was borrowed and blue and old."

Smacking sounds wafted through Liz's open window. Liz slid a glance over her shoulder. Lover Boy pursed his lips in an exaggerated kiss. The toothpick lifted.

"Borrowed?" asked Auntie.

Liz rolled her shoulder in dismissal of the teenage Romeo. Freeway flirtations. Only in L.A. "Yeah, he borrowed it from his second cousin."

Auntie eased on the brake, careful to stop a good twenty feet behind the Cadillac. "And never gave it back?"

"Well, his second cousin owed him a vacuum cleaner."

"Vacuum cleaner?"

"It had an arsenal of attachments, including one that could suck the grit out of—" she stopped herself from repeating Raven's colorful epithet "—uh, out of a ninety-degree corner. It was a gift for Raven's mother—he even purchased a special three-year warranty. Manfred borrowed the vacuum. Never gave it back."

Auntie blinked. "Manfred?"

Liz expelled a gust of air. The traffic, the heat, the kissing sounds were giving her a headache. "Yes, Manfred."

"Russell, Raven, Manfred. They don't sound as though they belong to the same family."

"Well, who can account for a family's differences? Look at you, Auntie. You're cultured, refined. Me, I'm—"

Auntie cut her off. "You're intelligent, hardworking, good-hearted. I know my special niece. I wouldn't be handing over this trust fund to just any relative, you know. You're my chosen one, my hope for the future." Her small hands tightened their grip on the wheel. "You were your daddy's darling, and deservedly so," she added softly.

Liz couldn't speak. *Daddy's darling.* After her mom's death when she was five, her dad had doled out enough love for two parents. "You're the joy of my life, dear heart," he'd say, giving her shoulder a squeeze. She could still hear the care in his voice—since his death, she'd often thought she'd never hear such tenderness again.

And then she met Russell.

She turned away, blinking back unexpected emotion.

Russell's voice that first night. She closed her eyes, remembering. He had quoted bits of poetry as though they were melodious offerings. Gifts of words that teased her mind and her heart. *Funny,* she thought, *similar to the gifts of words Auntie used to bring me.* Maybe the merging of a happy old memory with an exciting new experience was another reason she and Russell had clicked that first night. In so many ways, they had seemed so *right* together.

It had been as though she had spent a lifetime waiting for this man. This soul mate.

Smack. Smack.

Mr. Chevy Hormone. She huffed a release of air and opened her eyes, avoiding further macho-toothpick displays. "Get off here—it's the exit for the Rose," she said to Auntie, waving toward the next exit ramp.

With no warning, Auntie turned the wheel and cut in front of Lover Boy. He slammed on his brakes. A horn blared. A barrage of unintelligible words faded as they veered toward the exit.

"Ever hear of a turn signal?" Liz said quietly as they cruised to the first stoplight.

Auntie's lips curved in a slight smile. "Yes, but I thought I'd show that toothpick degenerate who's boss."

Liz did a slow turn and took in Auntie's determined profile. She was pretty cool, after all. Liz grinned. "You go, girl," she said admiringly.

Twenty minutes later, Auntie neatly parked the Audi in front of The Rose Tattoo. It took four parallel-parking attempts, but finally Auntie had maneuvered the car into place. Although Liz's idea of parking was to swerve and hit the kickstand, she didn't say a word. Instead, she tapped her crimson fingernails against the door's padded armrest and breathed in each time Auntie put the car in Reverse, out when Auntie moved forward again.

Not that Liz was into deep-breathing exercises. She just didn't want to overreact to Auntie's parking ritual, which probably had some unique superstitious significance, as well. After all, Auntie had just showed some guts cutting off the Toothpick Lothario.

Liz smiled at the recent memory as Auntie finally turned off the engine.

"I'll come in for a moment, sweetie," said Auntie, reaching for her ever-present pink handbag. "I need to make a phone call."

"Sure, Auntie." Liz swung open the car door and stepped onto the sidewalk. The heat of the concrete seeped through the bottoms of her sandals. July in L.A. She looked up at the haze that glazed the sky a brownish gray. This was the kind of hot, smoggy weather that made Angelenos pant and sweat.

Whatever the climate, Russell made her do both.

"Liz," called out a familiar masculine voice.

She looked back down. Through the heat-shimmering air she saw Dice, short for Paradise, ambling down the street with a stack of T-shirts draped over his arm. "Dice. Keeping cool?"

"Always cool, babe. Need a shirt?" He lifted his arm. "Got a special. Today only."

"Steak knives?"

"Earrings."

She grinned and waved him on. "No thanks."

"Dig it." He moved on and approached an older couple staring wide-eyed into the storefront window with the red-lingeried mannequin on all fours.

Only in L.A., Liz thought as she crossed to the front door of The Rose Tattoo. T-shirt vendors named Paradise. You'd think the guy would rather be in Hawaii or San Francisco or someplace more picturesque than in frantic, congested L.A. hawking his shirts.

She shoved her key into the lock, turned it and gave a swift kick to the bottom corner of the door. It opened with a sucking sound.

She walked into the cool, darkened room. But she knew why Dice stayed. Because L.A. had a funky character. If it was a person, it would wear rhinestone sunglasses, plaid shorts and tap shoes. Oh, yeah, that's why Dice stayed.

And why she stayed.

Auntie followed close behind as Liz walked into the room. "That young gentleman called you 'babe.'"

"He calls everyone 'babe.' Except guys."

Auntie stopped and clutched her purse waist-level. "He'd call me 'babe'?"

Liz turned on the overhead fan. It sputtered and creaked as it began to slowly rotate. "Only if you wanted."

"'Babe,'" Auntie repeated softly as though testing how the word felt in her mouth. "Years ago a young man called me 'baby.'" Her cheeks tinged pink. "But that was a long time ago. I suppose I wouldn't mind being called 'babe.' After all, I'm a nineties woman."

Seemingly pleased with her off-the-cuff logic, Auntie looked around. "Where's the phone?"

"Over there," Liz said, motioning to the small table next to the couch. She wondered if the young man who had called her Auntie "baby" was the same one who had stolen her heart. When Liz was young, Auntie would sometimes gaze into the distance and speak of him. What had been his name? Dan? No, David. She used to love to hear Auntie's sweet lilting voice say that name. Da-vid.

The name flowed like Russell. Russ-ell.

Russell.

Liz let her gaze linger on the answering machine for a moment. No blinking red light. No messages. He hadn't called.

Damn.

As Auntie tapped in her number, Liz tried to hide her disappointment. She busied herself getting ready for the night's customers. Checked her supplies. Turned on some soft-rock music. Flicked on the glass lamp, which infused the room with a colorful glow.

"The gloxinia convention is fully booked," enthused

Auntie as she hung up the phone. "My workshop on fertilizing is standing room only." She took mincing steps toward the stuffed wing-back chair in the center of the room. Sitting down, she carefully placed her handbag on the side table before turning to beam at Liz. "My first conference presentation." She blinked and jerked her head toward Liz. "But it's also your first important ceremony. Your *wedding*. I can't miss that!"

"Auntie, we've talked about this. It's going to be a simple Vegas chapel wedding. Just me, my man and probably some Elvis impersonator subbing for the minister—"

"They do that in Las Vegas?"

"Probably. Seriously, it's important for you to be a presenter. You've wanted this for a long time." *And I'd feel terrible if you miss it to watch me marry Raven, who isn't who you think I'm marrying and isn't who I would marry anyway if I was really getting married.*

Liz's thoughts made her dizzy. Like being on a crazy carnival ride. Better to focus on Auntie. "It's cool. Think of it as your turn to blossom. You'll be so good, I bet they'll name a gloxinia after you."

Auntie exhaled a deep breath. The lace on her bodice fluttered. "I think I have stage fright." Her blue eyes widened.

Looking at Auntie's childlike expression, filled with nervousness and excitement, Liz forgot all about her own misery. "You'll be dynamite," she said quietly.

She wanted to take her in her arms and cuddle her like a child. Speak softly to her and encourage her, assure her that no harm would come her way. Was this protective love what parents felt toward their children?

A sobering thought followed. *Someday I'll be like a mother to my aging auntie.*

Liz stepped away and opened the blinds on the window. Late-afternoon sun spilled into the room, stinging her eyes. She wished the rays would penetrate her soul and erase the pain. The idea of losing Auntie, her last family member, hurt. Pieces of her heart had been chipped away with the deaths of her parents. Would she even have a heart left after Auntie...

"You really think so?" Auntie asked.

"Think so?" Liz repeated mindlessly, blinking into the light.

"Think I'll be dynamite?"

Jolted back to the conversation, Liz swiped at her eyes and turned back around. "*Know* so," she said, forcing her voice to remain steady. "It's in our genes, my dear Auntie. We were born to be conference presenters."

For an instant, Auntie's face remained serious. Then she burst into a grin. "Born to be..." She shook her head and laughed, the sound light and lilting. "Born to be *babes*."

"And I'm born to be wild," boomed a deep voice.

They both turned and blinked at the mountain that blocked the open doorway.

"Oh!" Auntie exclaimed, sitting straighter. Her hands clasped the invisible handle of her handbag as though it sat in her lap. *A purse snatcher would have a hell of a time wrenching that handbag loose,* Liz thought.

"It's your future brother-in-law," Auntie said. "Ramon."

"Raven," Liz corrected.

"Raven. Yes," Auntie whispered.

Even though his shadow spilled across Auntie's face, Liz still caught her look of awe. Probably the only men Auntie interacted with on a daily basis were the mailman and grocer. Mild-mannered types with thinning hair and off-white button-down dress shirts. The opposite of Raven, a wild beast with a black braid and, today, a black T-shirt decorated with a white skull that had a bulging forehead. Underneath its skeletal smile were the words Brother Death.

Actually, the skull didn't have an oversize forehead, Liz realized on second glance. It was Raven's ham-size pecs that stretched the fabric over the skeletal brow.

He stepped into the room. As with all his T-shirts, the sleeves were ripped off so his Schwarzenegger arms could fit through. "Did I hear ya sayin' you were born to be a

babe?'' He turned slightly, exposing his iguana tattoo.
Streams of sunlight highlighted its bold primary colors.

Auntie nodded, her eyes darting from the iguana back to
the skull. "Brother Death? Is that what your friends call
you?"

He laughed, the sound more like a brewing storm than a
human's mirth. "Nah, sometimes my friends call me—"

Liz cleared her throat loudly and flashed Raven a warning look.

He hesitated. "They, uh, call me..." He shrugged self-
consciously. "Enjoy your shoppin'?"

Auntie nodded. "We purchased a wedding dress for Elizabeth. One that reflects her personality. Just as her dear
father, my brother, always said, she is her own fashion
statement."

Raven grinned. His silver bicuspid flashed. "That's my
lady. Uh, I mean my, uh..."

"Sister-in-law," said Liz crisply. Sheesh, she'd be glad
when this wedding was over and she could get on with her
life and school. She jerked her head in a come-here motion
to Raven.

"Excuse me, Auntie," he mumbled, crossing to Liz. The
floor shook with each step. The glass lamp rattled. Auntie
reached over and stilled it.

When he reached Liz, she poked the word "Brother" on
his T-shirt and hissed, "Watch what you say. Remember,
you're my brother-in-law-to-be—" She looked down.
"Why'd you wear your Brother Death shirt?"

"They didn't have a Brother-in-Law Death Shirt—"

"That's not what I meant." She rolled her eyes. "Don't
you have any T-shirts that have normal sayings?"

He looked down. "This is normal."

"Yeah. And my uncle was Elvis."

He jerked his head up. "He was?"

"No, he—oh, never mind."

"What are you two whispering about over there?"
Auntie asked, leaning a little in their direction.

Raven glanced back at her. "Was Elvis really your bro—"

"Raven," Liz interrupted loudly, "make yourself useful. Customers will start arriving soon." She didn't want Auntie thinking she was marrying into a family of loony tunes. If Auntie got overly concerned about Liz's future, she might withdraw her offer of the trust fund.

"Elvis?" Auntie asked, looking animated. "Is he really going to be the minister in Vegas?"

"Huh?" Raven frowned.

"Raven, sit. I have work to do." Marrying *into* a family of loony tunes? On second thought, she belonged to one.

Raven jerked his gaze around the room, which caused his skull-and-crossbones earring to swing back and forth. "Good idea. I'll go sit in my lookout chair. Play bouncer in case things get rough."

"Things get rough?" echoed Auntie.

Liz had been sashaying around the room, tidying up. Now she stopped and looked at Auntie, who appeared to be flushed with excitement. Maybe after all those years of being a librarian, Auntie was having the thrill of her life these past few days: naked men, Elvis as minister, the possibility of things getting "rough" in a tattoo parlor on Hollywood Boulevard. Beat gloxinias any day.

She crossed to Auntie's chair and patted her gently on the shoulder. *I should have kept more in contact these past few years,* Liz thought. *Given you more reasons to experience the "wilder" side of life.* She felt another surge of guilt that she had lied about the wedding in order to get the trust fund. *I'll make it up to you, Auntie. We'll spend more time together. Read together, just like in the old days.*

Liz glanced over her shoulder at the far corner of the room. A mammoth-size bookshelf, which she had positioned as a makeshift wall, shadowed the corner where Raven's "lookout chair"—actually a gray metallic folding chair—was located. He liked it. Called it his "bouncer hideout"—he'd jump in and scare the wits out of anyone bothering her or other customers. Fortunately, that didn't happen often.

The folding chair creaked. She knew he had sat down. Rustling sounds followed. "What's that?" Liz asked.

"Uh, bought some magazines today," replied Raven.

"Which ones?"

Silence. "Some, uh, wedding ones. To do research."

"You bought...bridal magazines?" she asked incredulously.

Raven grunted. "Like I said, doin' wedding research."

Auntie looked up and smiled benevolently at Liz. "Isn't that sweet? Wedding research. Your future brother-in-law treats you like family already."

Raven grunted.

"Oh!" Auntie exclaimed, looking toward the door. "Speaking of family, here's your fiancé."

The room went quiet.

Not a page rustled from the "bouncer lookout."

Please, God, no jealous-macho displays, Liz prayed. She slowly turned her head, wishing the butterflies in her stomach would stop their mad fluttering.

Russell.

He stood in the open doorway, perusing the room. Whereas Raven had blocked out the light, Russell basked in it. Golden rays clung to his form, accentuating nicely molded shoulders that tapered to trim hips. She'd never gotten a good look at his physique before. He was more athletic-looking than she recalled. Not a muscle-bound kind of guy, but one who was in shape. In good shape.

Damn, her palms were sweating. She pressed her hands against the coarse grain of her jeans, trying to stop herself from imagining more about Russell's body.

He stepped into the room, and she saw that he was nicely dressed. As though he was going to church. Shiny black dress shoes. Creased gray pants, matching gray jacket, buttoned. Shiny gray-speckled tie—the fancy kind she'd once seen in a store window in Beverly Hills.

Her gaze traveled up to his face.

Everything else might be gray coordinated, but his face was red.

Angry red.

Crossing his arms over his chest, he glared at Liz, then Auntie, then back at Liz.

"If you wanted to destroy me," he finally said in a low, measured tone. "Why didn't you just shoot me with a gun instead of with that damn camera?"

7

"DESTROY YOU?" Auntie repeated, the word *you* sliding into such a high range that Liz was certain dogs would come running.

Liz was accustomed to sometimes dealing with bawdy, drunken, unruly customers. She'd handled shattered windows, broken chairs and even a horse that a cop had backed through The Rose Tattoo's front door to avoid a wayward RTD bus. She viewed these incidents as minor job hazards but never disasters.

Until Russell. Every single day since he'd entered her life, there had been one near disaster after another.

And yet another one was beginning.

She had to do something. Fast. Before Raven's bouncer instincts kicked in.

Liz moved toward the front window and into the sunlight. Partially for warmth because she felt a sudden chill. And partially to divert Russell's attention.

It worked.

As he followed her every move, the anger in his eyes dimmed for a moment. Replaced by a look that she recognized from that first night when they met. A look of yearning. Passion, maybe. Not slap-together-bodies passion but something else. Something he seemed to be desperately longing for.

But the fleeting look disappeared, and his gray eyes once again sparked with anger.

"Here to return the pants?" she asked cautiously, knowing that was probably the last thing on his mind. But from her past experiences dealing with irate customers, she knew it was important to remain calm. Cool.

She looked over at Auntie, whose face was drained of color except for two perfect circles of rouge on her cheeks.

Liz returned her gaze to Russell. He stared at her with a fury that rivaled that of the highway patrolman who had once clocked her going over a hundred up Highway 1. Too bad Russell couldn't just give her a ticket and walk away.

"Forget the pants," she added, shrugging. "I'll buy George another pair."

"This isn't about pants," he said, enunciating each word.

"Customers will be arriving soon. Whatever happened to upset you, maybe we can discuss it later," she suggested.

"Whatever happened," Russell said, as though that was the strangest thing he'd ever heard. "What-ev-erhappened." He unfolded his arms and glanced from Auntie to Liz. "Let me guess." He tapped his forefinger theatrically against his temple. "You two have *no* idea what happened."

"Did that shirt vendor call *you* 'babe' too?" Auntie offered, seemingly eager to get to the heart of the matter.

Russell did a double take, then rocked back on his heels and lowered his head. "My life was normal before I met these people," he mumbled to the floor.

"What people?" Auntie asked, leaning forward, staring at the same spot on the floor.

Russell looked up. Auntie didn't.

"There's no one on the floor, Auntie," Liz said in a gentle aside.

Russell began pacing. It reminded her of that first morning-after on Hollywood Boulevard when he had carried on as though she hadn't given him a tat but the mark of the devil.

"How did I inherit these people?" he demanded to no one in particular. "I was living a normal life, minding my own business, and suddenly I'm clan to the Beverly Hillbillies."

Liz pressed her lips together to stop herself from smiling.

Russell's theatrics were...cute. But she knew better than to say so.

He halted and dragged a hand through his hair. She remembered those same fingers toying with her long hair, tugging gently on a strand to pull her closer. She fought the urge to lick her lips, to again taste his kiss.

His brow arched and he leveled her a piercing look.

Mmm. She liked that look. It went a little beyond cute. It looked downright sexy. A lock of hair had fallen across his brow, giving him a hint of a bad-boy aura. She liked it. Now it made sense where Max Harrington, the action-adventure screenwriter, came from.

"Am I in an alternative universe?" he said, gesturing broadly as though he had posed the question to a throng of observers. "Can somebody please answer me?"

The folding chair in the back creaked.

She'd better handle this before Raven went into action. "Russ, honey," Liz soothed, taking a step toward him. "Why don't we go out for a drink and talk about this."

He flashed her an incredulous look. "That's how all *this* started! You and me in a bar, sharing a drink. Remember? The symbolism of Yeats? I'll never again drink and spout poetry. When a man does that, he gets marked for life." He thumped his chest several times in quick succession.

Another creak.

Liz quickly crossed the room and stood squarely in front of Russell. "Hon, let's take a walk—"

"Walk? Why be so pedestrian. Let's take another gut-wrenching, mind-blowing ride on that Harley of yours. My hair could certainly use another wind-tunnel treatment." He swept the wayward lock of hair back into place, then turned his attention to Auntie.

"That's what happened the night of my bachelor party—a ritual that men for hundreds of years have participated in without their lives being ransacked, plundered and destroyed. But me? Oh, no-o-o-o. I have a bachelor party and end up with hair that has a will of its own, two women who think I'm going to marry them and leather pants that, if worn too long, could prove a viable alternative to a vasectomy.''

Auntie's thin lips pursed together. Her eyebrows arched so high that Liz thought they might touch her hairline.

"Russell," said Liz, "a walk—"

"A walk?" He glanced at her pants. "Aren't those a little tight?" He was frowning, giving her a once-over.

Nobody—especially no *guy*—ever criticized her appearance. Maybe she didn't dress like some Bel Air babe, but Liz knew she had the kind of body that looked great in anything. Last Halloween, dressed as a toaster, she had stopped traffic. She doubted even Demi Moore could have done that.

She placed one palm against her hip. "They fit fine—"

"Have you ever heard of breathing room?"

"I can breathe."

Russell jabbed his finger down his collar and craned his neck. "I can't. Maybe I shouldn't bother. Just stop breathing and ease into the next life." He closed his eyes. "Dear God, let me be reborn a monk."

Auntie fidgeted with the lace on her blouse. "Oh, you poor man." She looked anxiously at Liz. "Your fiancé must be getting the flu. He seems delirious."

Flu. Good idea. Now she knew how to get him out of here before he said something that cost her the trust fund.

She trailed a finger down his arm before gently cupping his elbow. "Flu. Poor baby. Let me put you to bed—"

Russell stared, mesmerized, at her trailing red fingernail. *Put you to bed.* Good Lord. This woman had the allure of a siren, the seductiveness of a mythological goddess, the body of a...

He swallowed hard. He wanted to hold on to his rage, but it dissipated into nothingness. In its place was a slow-burning need that emanated from the touch of her finger against his arm, seared through his skin and scorched a path straight to his libido.

"You need to be in bed," Liz said in a husky take-me voice. She was gently steering him out of the room and out the door. She could have steered directly into oncoming traffic and he would have willingly gone. The woman was a temptress extraordinaire.

Outside, the air swirled hot around them. Liz's flaming red hair lifted on a breeze and curled provocatively around her face.

That face. Had he ever really looked into those eyes before now? Sparkling green. Like the sea. A man could drown in those eyes, gladly.

"Where's your car?" she asked.

He could also drown in that voice. Like drowning in a vat of liquid honey.

"What are you thinking about, Russ?"

"Drowning."

"Okay. But let's get you in the car first. It's time for you to go home."

"I thought it was time for me to go to bed."

She cast him a sexy glance. "You're a stinker." She winked.

Desire rippled through him. Stinker. No woman, especially a first-class vixen, had ever called him stinker. It must rate up there with rake, scoundrel, heathen, animal...

"Car?"

He blinked. "Car?"

"You know...the thing with four wheels that you drove here?"

"Car! Of course. Yes, I know what one is."

"How about where you parked yours?"

"Right. Parked." He drew in a breath, pretending to think about his car when actually he wondered how she'd look peeled out of that sprayed-on outfit. "It's around here somewhere." But he didn't look around. Instead he stared into her exquisite face and wondered how it'd look against a pillow, staring up at him...

Her lips curled into a smile. "Blue Honda, right?" She looked up and down the street. "Down there. Behind the beige Toyota."

"I don't want to go." The confession shocked him. Not

that it wasn't the truth. It's just that he was accustomed to thinking before speaking. Around this woman, his passion easily wrestled control from his intellect.

She jutted out one hip and looked at him slyly. "Thought you were mad at me."

"I was. I am. We need to talk. About..."

"About?" she prodded.

Damn. He'd forgotten.

She smiled, as though knowing his brain cells had turned to mush. "I have to open my business. Tell you what, though. I'll drop by tomorrow morning and we'll talk about whatever's bothering you."

"We will?"

She nodded slowly, her red lips puckering slightly. "We'll make it a date—how's that?"

"A date?"

She chucked him playfully on the chin. "You need to loosen up, Professor. Yes, a date. And I'm going to give you the time of your life."

And with that, she turned on her heel and sashayed back into The Rose Tattoo.

RUSSELL AWOKE with a start. Blinking in the semidarkness, he turned and glanced at the digital clock. The red numbers indicated five-thirty. Five-thirty? He shifted his gaze to the window. The gray light of morning seeped through the blinds. Outside, birds chirped mercilessly. He doubted he'd ever seen the world at this ungodly hour. The birds could have it. He closed his eyes and settled back under the warm covers.

A honeyed voice played in his head. *"You need to loosen up, Professor... I'm going to give you the time of your life."*

His eyes popped open again.

Time of his life. A date. This morning.

With Liz.

He pressed his face against the pillow and groaned.

"And I forgot to ask at what *time* the time of my life begins."

Sometime this morning he had a date with the most luscious woman in the universe. He stared down the clock. Five-thirty-two. Should he call her? She might not like being wakened with the birds. She might hate it. She might tell him his untimely call turned her off and to forget it. One ill-timed phone call stood between him and the most cataclysmic, definitive, exotic time of his life.

Five thirty-three.

He'd wait until…seven. No, too early. Hollywood tattoo artists probably got to bed late. He'd call at eight.

But he couldn't lie here and watch the little red numbers change, minute by minute, for the next two-plus hours. He'd get ready now. It was about time he saw what all that chirping was about, anyway.

He sat up and pulled back the covers. Cool air assaulted his body. Looking down, he suddenly regretted that he was the type of man who wore boxers. To be truly worthy of La Liz, he should be the kind of stud who wore tiger-striped, stretchy, bulge-defining underwear.

"What am I thinking?" he croaked. *Almost-married men don't fantasize about redheaded vixens with bikini-perfect bodies who might catch a peek of his manly underwear.*

Except when the red-haired wild-blooded woman promised the time of his life. Which could be anything from a toboggan ride to…

Charlotte.

He squeezed his eyes shut and drew in a sharp breath.

He wouldn't—couldn't—do anything. Not to Charlotte and to their imminent union.

He opened his eyes and stared at the Toulouse-Lautrec print on his far wall. His gaze traveled up her bare back to her red hair caught in a chignon. He imagined loosening that hair and watching it fall, slowly, in long golden red curls against the woman's white skin.

But it wasn't the woman in the picture anymore. It was Liz.

He wanted this date. *What's one last virtual fling,* he rationalized. *I just want to be closer to her, to talk with her. No touching, no kissing. Nothing to be guilty about except the thoughts in my mind...*

The logic seemed sound. Reasonable. Charlotte would never know he was planning to rendezvous with the motorcycle heathen in the leather outfit that leaves nothing to the imagination.

To be on the safe side, he'd start the day with a cold shower.

An hour later, he sat in the living room, dressed in a pair of khaki slacks, a slightly worn T-shirt and a pair of white sneakers. The basic white T-shirt was at the other end of the T-shirt spectrum from Raven the Invincible, who seemed to own every counterculture black T-shirt ever made on this continent. In contrast, the white, Russell thought, was a positive image. In this neo-Western, Raven wore black, Russell wore white.

He glanced at his wristwatch. Seven. Still too early to call. No problem. He'd entertain himself until she arrived.

He tried to watch the news, but the newscasters' faces and words blurred as he imagined Liz and her silky red tresses and second-skin attire showing up any moment on his doorstep.

He tried to watch cartoons, but all the animated, goofy characters reminded him of himself preparing and waiting for the Harley Babe Goddess.

He had never carried on like this for Charlotte, he thought, flipping the channels for the zillionth time. No, everything with her had always been calm, collected, rehearsed. Their first date had been at the symphony. She often reminded him how he fell asleep between Brahms and Mozart.

Now here he was agitated and anxious between *Daybreak Report* and Daffy Duck.

A knock.

He jumped to his feet. "Be cool," he warned himself as he uncooly raced to the door and swung it wide open.

Her hand raised midknock, she look surprised. "That was fast," she said softly.

She was dressed in another ensemble that would make a leotard look like a muumuu. But he knew better than to make any more breathing-room comments. "I walk faster in the mornings."

"Oh." She dropped her hand. A confused look flitted across her face.

Her face. Sea green eyes that a man would gladly drown in. Full, pouty lips that promised long, hot, lingering kisses...

An image of Charlotte flitted through his brain, but it was hazy, distant. A tickling of guilt edged into his consciousness.

It's a virtual date, he reminded himself. *Innocent. Okay, not as in pure as the driven snow. More like slightly dirty slush. But it's my last chance to feel crazy, out of control. My last chance to be with Liz for the rest of my life...*

Liz cocked her head. "What are you thinking about, Russell?"

"Snow."

"In L.A.?" She paused. "In July?"

"Make that slush. Not snow. I was thinking of slush."

She nodded once, slowly. "Right. Shall we take off?"

"Take off what?"

She frowned slightly, then her lips pursed as she obviously fought to suppress a grin. "Not what, *where.*"

"Where." He digested the word. "Of course. *Where.*" He clapped his hands together and rocked back on his heels. "Have no idea why I said 'what.'" He stared upward before looking back down. "Okay, I confess. Maybe I do know. Has to do with the snow-slush theme from before, but we can skip particulars. Sorry I'm acting like such an idiot, but your beauty erases all the benefits of an advanced education, causing me to devolve into some kind of primal being who forgets how to maintain a civilized conversation."

A slight blush rouged her cheeks. She smiled again, with

a hint of self-consciousness this time. "You're saying I look nice. Thank you, Russell. Oh!" she exclaimed, handing him a small pink coin purse. "Would you mind tucking this into your pocket? It's too lumpy to fit into mine."

His eyes dipped to her slim, shapely hips. He doubted she could even slip a thin dime into those pants pockets. "Sure," he answered, but it came out more like a strangled bark. He grabbed the coin purse and shoved it into his pocket.

"You're wearing mismatched socks," she said incredulously.

He looked down. Over the tops of his sneakers he saw one white sock, one argyle sock. Charlotte would be halfway into a sartorial fit right now. "I'll change—"

"No." Liz giggled. "It's cool. I like it. Goes with your devolved, primitive personality." She winked saucily, turned and bounded down the steps. "Come on, Mr. Socks. Let's start this day with some of the wickedest java you've ever wrapped your lips around."

They rode her Harley down to Santa Monica Pier, where she parked in front of a shack with the words Wicked Brew stenciled in a coffee-bean alphabet on its front window. Inside, the aroma of roasted coffee was overpowering. Russell swore he had a caffeine buzz just sniffing the air and reading the myriad coffee types that covered an entire wall.

"Try Java Jalapeño," suggested Liz.

"No way."

"It'll put hair on your chest."

"Got enough, thanks." He caught her sideways glance.

"Live a little," she murmured.

Maybe it was the smoky Lauren Bacall quality of her voice. Maybe it was the suggestive look in her eyes. But he caved in and eventually, when he finally sipped "the wickedest java you've ever wrapped your lips around," decided that the steamy and spicy Java Jalapeño was quite good.

Steamy and spicy. Like Liz.

Afterward, as they ambled down the boardwalk, Russell

heard the chink-chink of Liz's coin purse in his pocket. It took all his willpower not to stare at her spray-on pants that had no room except for her compact body.

"It's a small room," Liz suddenly said.

He felt the heat rise from his chest to his neck. "Pardon?"

"Yolks," she explained, motioning to a coffee shop they were approaching. "It's a cramped, one-room joint, but it's got killer eggs."

They walked inside. It was small, all right. "A wanna-be coffee shop," Russell whispered to Liz. The walls were painted wake-up yellow. Yolks didn't have a menu. Instead, from behind the cash register, a beefy guy wearing a po-nytail announced that today's special was big chunky fries and eggs "any way you like 'em."

Liz leaned over to Russell. "That's always the special."

After they ordered, the beefy guy told a string of chicken-crossing-the-road jokes while he cooked their order on the grill.

Liz nudged Russell. "Yolks. Get it? He came to L.A. to be a comic."

"And ended up a chunky-fries-egg guy?"

"On the pier, he's a star."

"He shouldn't have dreamed."

Liz did a double take at Russell but said nothing.

They ate their breakfasts at a counter that faced large open windows. While inhaling the salty, tangy sea air, they wolfed down their fries and eggs. Scrambled for him, over easy with green chili for her.

"I know you picked Liz for Elizabeth Barrett Browning," he said, spearing a forkful of egg. "But I think you should be named Spicy."

"Because I like green chili?"

"And Java Jalapeño." *And because you're one hot vixen babe.*

Dabbing a fry at the last of her eggs, she said, "Well, next, Spicy would like to ride horses. I got dibs on the fuchsia stallion with the gold saddle."

He set his fork on the plate. "Beg your pardon?"

She leaned an elbow on the counter and cast him a dreamy look. "Tell me the kind of horse you like to ride."

"One with four wheels and brakes?"

She leaned closer. Her exotic perfume mingled with the sea breezes. The lethal combination swirled through his brain, igniting thoughts that were hotter than a double dose of Java Jalapeño.

She playfully pointed a red fingernail at him. "They're not real, silly. Carousel horses. Describe the kind you'd like to ride." She gave him a penetrating look. "Or don't you like to dream?"

"Dream?" He wadded up his paper napkin and tossed it on his plate. "I do it most nights."

"I mean dreams about your future. Things your heart wishes for."

He felt his insides chill. Her lighthearted question was innocent, but it triggered bad memories, nevertheless. "I'm not a dreamer, if that's what you're asking," he answered solemnly.

A breeze lifted her hair slightly. Pulling a strand away from her face, she said, "Did I say something to upset you?"

He didn't want to ruin this day. Best to brush it off. "I'm just not one to dream, that's all."

"I am!" She said it with such conviction that he was a little taken aback. "What else is life about if you don't dream?"

A lot.

Lowering her voice, Liz continued. "Auntie and I used to read fanciful stories together when I was a little girl. I suppose that's when my dreams started. And then when Dad died, it became more important than ever to fulfill my dreams *now* and not wait, because what if there isn't a tomorrow?"

He aimlessly traced a crack in the counter's Formica top. "I'm sorry…about your father."

She touched his hand lightly. "It's okay. It's been eleven

years. I nursed him from the time I was fourteen until his death when I was sixteen. Guess I did a lot of thinking during that time...about what life is...what dreams are..."

Her voice faded as she stared out at the ocean. "Dad never allowed himself to dream. And because of that, he ended up living half a life. I swore I'd be different. I'm going to grab life like a brass ring and go for my dreams."

Dreams again. He stared at her determined profile. "So that's what this trust fund is about?"

She nodded. "For me, yes."

"And Auntie?"

Her gaze wavered. "Auntie wants me to settle down and raise a family. A few years ago, she told me this trust fund was mine if I married by my twenty-seventh birthday."

"Twenty-seven. Is that some kind of prime settling-down age?"

"As you know..." Liz turned her head and smiled. "Auntie has a superstitious streak. Not in any conventional way—you know, black cats, salt over the shoulder, that kind of stuff. But in her own unique way, she's superstitious. I think this age thing, twenty-seven, is because she was to be married on her twenty-seventh birthday. But the wedding was postponed."

Straightening, Liz crossed her arms. "I'm guessing, but I think my guess is right on. She thinks that if I don't get hitched by that magic-number birthday, I'm doomed to live the life of a spinster."

He looked into Liz's come-hither eyes and soft, luscious lips that, he remembered, tasted warm, moist and a little like honey. "I seriously doubt you'll ever end up a spinster."

She smiled her thanks.

"But won't Auntie get a little confused seeing you marry Raven after introducing me as your fiancé?"

Liz uncrossed her arms. "She won't be there—she's going to a gloxinia convention. Which she'd probably skip if she wasn't a presenter for the first time. She's scared half to death, but it's her dream come true."

More dreams. "Scared?"

"She was a librarian for years and years. She's more comfortable hiding behind books than speaking to people."

The husky tenor of Liz's voice made sitting very uncomfortable. He wished he had a stack of books to hide behind right now. "So, uh, why didn't Auntie get married?"

She blinked. "It's a sad story. They fell in love during the war and got engaged. My dad told me they were 'besotted' with each other. After the war ended, they planned to marry on her twenty-seventh birthday, as I told you. But David—her fiancé—wanted to wait until he'd finished law school and socked away some money. So they postponed the wedding. A few years later, he died in a car accident. In his will he left everything to her—every single penny he'd saved. She kept it all these years…" Her voice trailed off.

"And that's the trust fund," Russell said softly.

"Yes." Liz curled a strand of hair around her finger. "Or, I think so. When Auntie sprung this trust fund idea on me a few years back, I asked her where the money came from, but she didn't want to discuss 'particulars.' Actually, she hasn't wanted to discuss the past or David for many, many years…"

She sighed and dropped her hand to the countertop. "Dear sweet Auntie. I'm not trying to be deceitful, you know."

"About what?"

"About faking a marriage. It's just that I have this chance, *now,* to go to college. To be more than a tattoo artist, you know? And someday, when I marry the right person, well, I hope Auntie understands."

The right person. He tried to imagine who that would be for Liz. Someone in a Raven mold, no way. She deserved a man who appreciated her for more than her beauty and obvious sensuality. She was bright, determined, creative.

And he didn't want another man to have her.

He blew out a gust of air and searched the skyline. In

the distance the gray ocean rolled and tossed in white frothy caps—turbulent, the way his soul felt.

"What's the matter?" asked Liz.

He couldn't change the way things were. He was marrying Charlotte. And, down the road, Liz would find herself, and then her own husband. Today would be a memory. A wonderful memory. But nothing more.

"Let's find that pink horse with the shiny saddle," he said, avoiding the question.

She narrowed her eyes. "Fuchsia stallion with the gold saddle."

"Dreamer."

Her eyes widened. She grinned. "You got that right."

The carousel, a few minutes walk from Yolks, was halfway down the pier. The pervasive scent of salty sea air followed them inside. The morning sun slanted in through the tall vertical windows of the building, casting rectangular boxes of yellow light on the hardwood floor.

The carousel stood in the middle of the room. On it, in the midst of other colorful horses, was the fuchsia stallion with a gold saddle.

Liz tossed her hair over her shoulder. "And you doubted me? Sometimes dreams do come true, you know. Loosen up and live a little, Max."

Max. She was teasing him with his own dream of being Max Harrington, screenwriter. A dream he'd never fulfill. After all, who in Hollywood didn't want to be something—an actor, a screenwriter, a whatever? Even that guy at Yolks had wanted a piece of stardom.

They reached the ticket booth and Russell pulled out her coin purse, then returned it to his pocket. "My treat." Extracting his wallet, he added, "I'm content being a professor and building a literary criticism career." It had slipped out. But he heard the edge of defensiveness in his voice.

"Right," Liz answered wryly.

The fleshy woman in the booth took his dollar and pushed back two orange ticket stubs and two quarters. A cigarette burned in a glass ashtray at her elbow. "Have fun, kids," she said in a throaty growl.

Liz watched Russell pocket the change. Didn't he realize that contented men don't go chasing after other women? He knew as well as she that what they shared was exciting, thrilling, a once-in-a-lifetime thing. A dream come true.

But then, for some reason, he didn't believe in dreams. Or didn't trust himself to dream.

"Come on," urged Liz. "Let's pick out a wild stallion for you."

He frowned and hesitated. "I'll just take one of those nicely bolted down benches." He nodded toward a purple-and-green one that sat in between two of the horses.

Liz grabbed his hand and gave it a tug. "You're not benching it, Max. This is the time for you to pick the wildest, meanest stallion in the bunch. The kind a hot-stuff Hollywood action-adventure screenwriter would ride to work."

She hopped onto the carousel platform, pulling him with her. They were the only two there, making it their private playground. Next to the ticket booth, a gray-haired fellow leaned his wiry frame against a lever, waiting to start the ride.

Liz walked among the horses, running her fingers over their smooth, ornate forms until she chanced upon a black stallion with a bronze-and-red saddle. An oversize jewel—an emerald, she decided—decorated its massive black forehead.

"I found it," she called out.

Russell sidled into view, eyeing the inanimate beasts warily. "Really, I'm more the bench type—"

She ignored him and slapped the horse's rump. "This is your baby. I think we should name him Sylvester. As in Stallone. The Italian Stallion—get it?"

"Why not Arnold?"

She thrust her index finger into the air as a thought hit. "I have a much better idea. Let's name him…Dream Boy!"

Russell hesitated. "I don't think so."

"Yes," she enthused. "Dream Boy. Just like—"

"I'm not a dreamer."

"Not even for one day? One ride?" She patted the saddle. "Who asked you out, anyway? I think you owe it to Spicy to loosen your imagination a little."

She looked him up and down. Loosening was a great idea—but she wouldn't pursue that one. She might be hotter for him than a match to a firecracker, but she didn't make moves on another woman's man. Even if the woman was absolutely wrong for the guy.

"I promise not to take a picture," Liz added. "No one will ever know about this day, except for me."

A funny look crossed his face. "About...pictures," he said thoughtfully. "That one Auntie took—"

Liz waved his comment aside. "Oh, Auntie. Another of her superstitions. Her second cousin took a picture of her and David the day they got engaged. She got it into her head that the picture sealed their fate as lovers. Or so she once said."

The thought saddened her. She glanced toward the ticket booth and watched the woman, who was leaning out the side door of the booth as she smoked and talked to the older fellow. "Maybe Auntie was right. Maybe that picture sealed their fate. She never loved another man. Ever."

When she glanced back, the look in Russell's eyes had softened. "I hadn't realized..." he murmured. But he didn't finish his thought.

Their eyes held. At this moment Russell seemed open. Vulnerable. As though he were dropping his guard and letting her in. It reminded her of that first night when they'd met. She wondered if Charlotte ever took the time to see into Russell's soul, to understand the dreams he hid from the world.

"Why are you afraid to dream?" she asked softly.

Russell gave his head a shake. "Not now, Liz—"

"I want to know."

"You kids gonna ride or talk all day?" called out a grumpy male voice.

Liz looked over. The old man gripped the lever and squinted at them.

Russell chuckled. "Looks like I gotta take Dream Boy to work or I'll be late."

Laughing, Liz ran to her fuchsia stallion, hopped on, then gave the fellow a thumbs-up.

The rest of the day was spent in different parts of L.A. They sauntered through Pacific Palisades Park, enjoying the panoramic view of the Pacific Ocean. Afterward, Liz announced an expedition to her "fave" pizza parlor in all of L.A. (Later, while they ate, Russell thanked her for not ordering his with jalapeño.) They spent the afternoon strolling along Melrose Avenue—where Russell saw more body parts pierced than he knew possible ("That girl has her lip, nose and eyebrow pierced—how many sets of earrings does she have to buy?") Such comments made Liz laugh. They also made her realize how, despite his imagination, he seemed sheltered from the world. As though he held back from experiencing life.

The same way he held back from experiencing his dreams?

Around six, as the sun lowered in the west, Liz pulled up in front of Russell's apartment building. They sat for a moment, their bodies close.

Russell slowly released his hold on her waist. "I think your Harley needs a name," he said mischievously, getting off her bike.

"Sylvester? Arnold?" She tried to sound lighthearted, but her insides were caving in. She'd never see Russell again. Or, if she did, he'd be married to another woman.

"No." He lingered on the strip of grass next to the sidewalk, his face lightly tanned from the day in the sun. "You should name your bike Dream Girl."

Liz smiled. "Knew I'd get to you, Max. Dreams are good, you know."

"For some, maybe," he conceded.

She wished he'd lean over and kiss her. Press his warm lips against hers and murmur some of the sweet nothings just as he had that first night. She imagined feeling his sun-warmed cheek against hers. Inhaling his woodsy cologne.

But he didn't make a move. No doubt being good. As was only right. Inwardly, she released the fantasy. At least she would always have the memory of their spending this day together.

"Dream Girl it is, Max." She smiled. Or tried to. Stepping on the gas, she steered the bike back onto the road and roared away.

Russell watched her until she turned the corner and left his sight. He suddenly felt empty. And terribly alone. He turned around and started up the walk to his building.

Chink. Chink.

He stopped and placed his hand over his pants pocket.

8

HE SURPRISED AUNTIE when he strolled into The Rose Tattoo thirty minutes later.

"Oh, hello!"

"Hello. I, uh, came back to return Liz's coin purse."

"She's in the other room. Shall I call her?"

"No, it's nice to talk with you for a few minutes."

Auntie clasped her small white hands together. "Elizabeth looked positively radiant when she got in. You two lovebirds must have had some day." Her eyes twinkled.

He was speechless. Some part of him liked hearing that he and Liz were "lovebirds," although, in truth, they would soon be flying in different directions. Different lives.

Auntie peered more closely at him, looking concerned. "Oh, you got some sun," she said. "Be careful. You want to be healthy on your wedding day."

"Yes, I do," he answered quietly. *I do.* Vows he'd be sharing with another. He had to pacify this agony in his gut. Charlotte was the woman he was marrying. Liz was…Liz was a momentary thrill. A taste of spice. But even he couldn't consume jalapeños every day of his life.

"Auntie, you need to know something."

A chair creaked. He glanced back into the shadows but didn't see anything.

"Max!"

He looked to the side and watched Liz enter the room.

"Long time," she teased, then stopped and stared at him. Maybe he was happy to see her a short while ago, but right now he looked as though someone had died.

"Liz," he said slowly, "We can't keep lying to Auntie."

Another creak.

"Please, no. Don't," Liz murmured.

She didn't dare look back at Raven, who was sitting on the folding chair in his "hiding spot" at the back of the room. He might misinterpret it as a plea for help. Behind her, she waved at him to stay put. That is, if he even bothered to look at her frantic signal. No doubt Raven was staring down Russell, just waiting for the opportunity to play bouncer.

"Liz, it's not fair to her," he continued. "After all she's gone through. After all she's done for you, it's time to square things."

"Like hell," an ominous voice grumbled.

Everyone looked toward the back of the room.

A dark bulky shape rose in the corner.

Russell stared stone-faced at the growing shadow. "Wonderful. A haunted tattoo parlor."

Heavy steps shook the floor as Raven stepped forward into the light.

"The Ghost of Dinner Past," murmured Russell.

Raven drew in a slow, deep breath. The skull's eye sockets swelled to twice their size. He twisted the magazine he was reading into a tight roll.

Staring at the magazine, Russell raised his hand to his throat.

Raven, looking like a Hefty bag with feet, crossed the room and slammed to a dead stop in front of Russell. The Fu Manchu mustache quivered as Raven spoke. "You gonna apologize to the ladies before you go."

Russell stared straight ahead, nose to nose with the skull's empty nose hole.

"Raven," said Liz, forcing herself to speak evenly. "No need to practice your bouncer techniques on Russell. He's leaving."

Raven stared down at the top of Russell's head. "The dude ain't apologized yet."

"Oh, my, did you two boys fight like this growing up?" asked Auntie in a tremulous voice.

"One of us didn't grow up," Russell replied.

Raven puffed out his chest even more. Russell's nose disappeared into the black T-shirt.

"What's that supposed to mean—one of us didn't grow up?"

"It means," answered Russell in a muffled voice, "that although your body has aged, your mind hasn't."

Raven's brows pressed together as he seemed to mull over the words. Liz had often thought that reality usually hit Raven several seconds—sometimes minutes—after everyone else. She started to interrupt when Raven suddenly bellowed.

"My body's in great shape!" He stepped back to flex his arm in an exaggerated bodybuilder pose and popped his biceps, causing the iguana to slither. He then hurtled forward, barely missing the glass lamp, and grasped Russell by the shirt.

A long, ripping sound followed.

Auntie squealed, and cupped her white hands to her whiter face.

Liz groaned.

Everyone stared at Raven, who held half of Russell's T-shirt.

"That's it!" Liz yelled, stomping into the middle of the floor and holding up both hands in a traffic-stopping gesture. Reaching Raven, she steadied him with one hand while continuing to speak.

"I can't believe that you—" she eagled-eyed Russell "—and you—" she leveled a glance at Raven "—are acting like two overtestosteroned teenage boys."

Liz put her hands on her hips and continued her lecture. "Fortunately, one of you didn't ram your foot through a wall or shove a fist through the front window. Or, God forbid, land on Auntie. But that doesn't mean damage hasn't been done." She gestured toward the front window. "I've probably lost customers who looked in, saw you two carrying on and left."

Hot tears stung the corners of her eyes. She was worried

about losing her dream? She was going to lose her bread and butter with these guys' antics. "I want you both out," she said between gritted teeth. "Before you destroy my only means of making a living."

No one moved.

"Out!" She pointed her red-tipped finger toward the front door. She hoped they didn't see that her hand was shaking.

Auntie slowly rose from her chair.

"Not you, Auntie," Liz said in a quavering voice.

"No, dear, I know." Auntie gave Liz one of those benevolent smiles. "I just wanted to suggest that you boys—" she dipped her white head toward Russell, then Raven "—go out to dinner, have a few beers, make up. After all, you're both in the wedding party in a few days. This is no time for family feuds."

Russell, who was still staring at his half a T, bolted to attention. "We need to clear the air and stop these ridiculous charades."

As if he were Frankenstein's monster come to life, the light returned to Raven's beady eyes. Focusing his attention on Russell, he growled.

"Liz, call off your guard dog so I can finish what I was saying." He looked at Liz. "Can't you marry someone else? Surely you don't need me. I'll make it easy for you." He touched his chest. "Forget the tattoo…I'll wear T-shirts for the rest of my life." He glanced at Raven. "Tasteful T-shirts, hopefully. Just please find someone else to marry so I can get on with my life."

Auntie got up and crossed to Russell. "You poor man," she said, touching his arm lightly. "It's only cold feet. All grooms-to-be get them, I've heard."

"No, Auntie. Not cold feet. The Madays have seen the picture you put in the paper and it's going to take every ounce of my persuasive abilities to grovel my way back into their good graces."

"Who are the Madays?" Auntie asked, looking at Liz in bewilderment.

Russell followed Auntie's gaze.

His stomach plummeted when he saw Liz's face.

"So that's what happened," she said softly.

She looked crushed. Totally unlike the self-assured, sometimes brazen Liz he had come to know. Her lithe body bordered on frail, as though she were a child masquerading as a woman. Her flaming red hair tumbled loosely about her pale face. Even across the room, he saw how her lips trembled.

Remorse shot through him.

Because he was destroying her dream.

In his selfishness, he had forgotten how important dreams were to her. Maybe he had given up on his, but she hadn't given up on hers.

She absently wiped one hand across her eyes, as though to erase what had just transpired.

He wanted to reach out. Say something. But her despair left him speechless. It was bad enough watching his own life crash and burn, but now he'd inflicted the same tragedy on another's life. This wasn't Charlotte who had family money to buoy her through any calamity. This was Liz, Elizabeth, who had had to fight for everything she owned.

To destroy such a woman's dream was tantamount to willfully committing a sin.

He reached toward her. "Liz—"

"I'll explain everything to you later, Auntie. But for now, I think Mr. Harrington needs to leave." She covered her face with her hand.

"Lizzy," Raven said in a wounded voice. His shoulders sank. His chicken-size hands hung helplessly at his sides. "Don't cry. It's gonna be okay."

She dropped her hand. "Just leave me alone," she whispered hoarsely. "Everyone, leave me alone." She blinked back the tears that welled in her eyes.

Russell rubbed his thumb along his jaw. How could he ever make amends? At this moment, he'd give anything to turn back time and erase his thoughtless words.

He glanced around the room. It seemed they were all at

a loss as to what to do for Liz. Maybe because they'd never seen strong, capable, independent Liz hurting so deeply.

Auntie's powdered face was pinched with worry as she stared at her niece crying. "Dear heart," she murmured softly, over and over. "It will be all right, dear heart."

A dark cloud passed overhead. And stayed.

"Nobody makes my Lizzy cry."

Raven stood in front of him. It was bad enough having those bullet-hole eyes boring into him, but the skull's cavernous eyes made it seem as though Russell was facing a gallery of accusers.

For a millisecond, he thought of discussing this rationally with Raven. After all, Russell never meant to create this situation. His intentions had been selfish but not cruel.

But one didn't explain such things to a man whose pecs were a triple D.

Time for action.

Russell checked his peripheral vision to see how many running steps to the front door.

He bolted for freedom.

Once outside The Rose Tattoo, he skidded to a stop and blinked at the blinding sun.

Rays of light speared through the smoggy early-evening L.A. sky and stabbed at his eyes. Along Hollywood Boulevard, traffic whizzed by. Damn. His car keys were in his torn-to-bits T-shirt. He always dropped his keys in his pants pocket, but because Liz's coin purse was there, he'd plunked his keys in his T-shirt pocket after getting out of the car.

Which he'd driven here because he wanted to deliver the coin purse, which he hadn't had a chance to do.

So now he had no keys, but he still had the purse.

Life wasn't fair.

Life would also be short if he didn't quickly plan an escape route from Brother Death.

"Man, you look ready for another free T."

Jerking his gaze away from the light, Russell spied the pudgy vendor, his arms loaded down with T-shirts.

"I'm going to die," Russell said matter-of-factly. He quickly looked down both sides of the street, debating which way to run.

"Who isn't," answered the T-shirt man.

Probably moonlights as a Death Row counselor, Russell thought, pivoting east, toward Western Avenue. He could jog a good mile or two—okay, a quarter mile—then, using his calling card, he'd phone Drake to pick him up.

Plan set, Russell took a jumping step to the left.

And froze.

Just because his life was on the line, he couldn't afford to behave irrationally. A half-naked man running frantically down Hollywood Boulevard would receive the wrong kind of attention in this part of town.

"Here's a cheery one." Mr. T-shirt unfurled a white cotton shirt that read Bop Until You Drop in bright purple letters.

Bop? At least he wouldn't be bare-chested. He grabbed the shirt.

"Bop. Fifties lingo. 'Member?" The vendor picked something off his front tooth.

"I wasn't born yet."

"Too bad. You missed poodle skirts."

Russell yanked the shirt over his head and shoved his arms through the sleeves. "Gotta go."

"Got a special on earrings—"

"Don't wear them."

"No prob."

Prepared to run faster than Speedy Gonzales after a double espresso, Russell started to dart away when something warm and solid touched his back. He froze middart, knowing in his gut what he felt.

A hand.

The hand of death.

Brother Death.

Any instant, Raven's fist would crash through Russell's back, tear through his rib cage and extract his heart, still beating, from his chest. And Charlotte worried about mismatched socks? Tomorrow's papers would show English professor and literary critic Russell Harrington sprawled in a pool of blood on Hollywood Boulevard, nattily dressed in a Bop Until You Drop T-shirt.

Another picture for the Madays to add to their growing collection. That itself was a fate worse than death.

If he only had a few seconds to live, he'd make the best of it. Even if his legacy was a humiliating photograph, his last words would be memorable. Noble.

"Bop Until You Drop!" he yelled, thrashing at the air. "Bop Until—"

"Russell, be cool. It's me." Liz squeezed his shoulder.

He pivoted, his breath coming in ragged gulps.

"Told ya that shirt would cheer you up," said the vendor, nodding affirmatively. He winked at Liz. "Just a minute ago, he said he was going to die. Now he wants to bop. The magic of T-shirts. Gets 'em every time."

"Dice, could you check on Auntie?" asked Liz sweetly.

"Auntie?" Russell craned his neck to look through the window of The Rose Tattoo. It looked as though Auntie was sitting on top of a large black refrigerator. "What's she doing?" he asked incredulously.

"Riding piggyback on Raven," Liz said, extracting a key from her back pocket.

"She's an elderly woman," Russell said, unable to fathom why—or even how—a woman her age had ascended Mt. Raven. "She'll get hurt."

Liz motioned for Russell to follow her. "Raven's attempting to talk her down. He wouldn't hurt her for the world. She's playing the clinging vine, though, so we can make our great escape, so let's do just that..." She looked at Dice. "Help Auntie and contain Raven, will you?"

He gave his beret a tug and faced The Rose Tattoo. "No prob. Paradise to the rescue." He headed inside, holding his T-shirts in front of him. "Comin' in, Rave. Stay cool, brother."

"He must be crazy," muttered Russell, following Liz. "Going in there armed with T-shirts."

"You must be crazy. Yelling 'Bop Until You Drop.'"

"I panicked."

"Mr. English Professor panicked? Aren't you the guy who mouths Yeats at the drop of a hat?"

"That's when I'm feeling immortal. When you think you have only seconds to live, short-term memory kicks in."

They reached her Harley. Parked at the curb, it looked like some New Age metallic creature. Sunlight glinted along the chrome. The long beaded lever fringes fluttered with the rush of passing traffic.

"Hop on," ordered Liz as she swung one slim leg over the driver's saddle. "It's still rush hour," she grumbled, shoving the key into the ignition. "Driving in this is gonna be a bi—" The engine's roar drowned the rest of her words.

Here I go again. Russell settled behind her and grasped her tiny waist. He couldn't tell if his body was shaking from fear or gyrating in time with the engine's ear-shattering rumble. His head jerked back as the Harley shot into traffic.

With great effort, he leaned forward and pressed himself against Liz's back. Air rushed around his body. His T-shirt snapped like a flag on a windy day. A car honked as the Harley swerved into another lane. Jeez, Liz was a terror on the streets.

He pressed closer to the terror's back.

She was wearing some kind of stretch top that clung to her like a second skin. Through his thin cotton T-shirt and her body-hugging sheath, he could feel her slim form. Slim and muscled. How did she stay fit? Tattooing?

She flicked a look over her shoulder and veered into the far lane. As she maneuvered the bike, he noticed how her shoulder muscles shifted. She had what bodybuilders called "definition."

Or that's what he thought they called it. Although "definition" to him applied to words in a dictionary, he'd heard the same term used in some movie or TV show. Or maybe from Drake, who loved to describe the female species in long, rambling soliloquies.

Female species. He, Russell, was right at this moment riding with the Queen of the Female Species, their bodies one with the machine that reverberated and rumbled between their legs.

He dropped his head back and drank in the rush of sky and air. Lord, oh Lord. *I'm tearing down Hollywood Boulevard, racing for my life from Refrigerator Man. A tattoo on my chest. A woman in my arms.*

"Move over, Brad Pitt!" he yelled into the wind. "I'm on a roll!"

"You okay?"

She was looking at him in her rearview mirror. "Okay," he mouthed, and smiled. Or attempted to smile. The onslaught of air made his upper lip flap uncontrollably. He held it down with his bottom teeth and nodded affirmatively.

Riding on Harleys must do something to normal human beings. He had to contain himself and remember that they were in escape mode, not Brad Pitt mode.

"Hold on," she commanded.

He tightened his grip around her waist. Her small, firm waist. A waist that definitely had definition.

He shifted his fingers slightly, trying to memorize the indentation of her form. How her slim middle flared slightly to the hips. He imagined how it would feel to stroke her soft skin and explore her body's silky terrain. To delve into the crevices, to trace the contours...

They rumbled to a stop at an intersection. Russell stared at the red light. Its crimson glow seared through his brain, illuminating a fantasy of two bodies, intertwined, writhing in a heated embrace. The woman's taut form molded against his. They fitted perfectly, like two pieces of a puzzle.

He mentally stepped into the fantasy. He was now holding the woman. He lifted her chin with his finger and looked into Liz's half-closed eyes. In the ruby glow, he caught the seductive glimmer of need in her gaze. She nestled closer. Her long hair, glinting scarlet and gold, crushed against his chest, burning his skin. Parting her lips, she offered him a kiss. He leaned down and tasted her...

Whoa. He had to stop staring at the stoplight.

He shifted in his seat and looked to the side. The older gentleman in the Buick next to him peered cautiously out his closed window. The man's horn-rimmed glasses raised slightly as he scanned Liz's skintight turquoise jeans. Then he looked at Russell.

As the light turned green and the Harley rolled forward, Russell caught the man mouthing the word "Bop," a confused look on his face.

Too bad, buddy. You missed poodle skirts, Russell thought, congratulating himself on his recent history lesson.

As they careened forward, the scent of Liz's perfume—exotic, spicy—flowed over him. He had the irrational thought that he could spend the rest of his days like this, roaring through life, his senses overloading on the rushes of air, exotic perfume and the feel of Liz's compact body.

A life on the edge, that's what he was living at this very moment. Forget Brad Pitt. He was Max Harrington, action-adventure screenwriter, burning a path through life like a blazing meteor through the sky.

The bike slowed to a stop at the next light.

Catching his breath, Russell edged forward. Touching his cheek against Liz's, he asked, "Where are we going?" If she had said Straight to heaven, he would have believed her. He would go anywhere, follow her to the ends of the earth, if need be.

She turned slightly and their lips almost touched. "Santa Monica," she said, her voice breathy. She quickly angled her head away. "You haven't moved since this afternoon, have you?" In the blink of an eye, her voice had changed. No-nonsense. Terse.

"Right. Santa Monica," he murmured. So much for the ends of the earth. He'd have to settle for the outskirts of L.A.

But despite her changed tone, he had caught the look in her eyes. That narrow, seductive gaze as though she were fantasizing about him, too. The same look he had seen in his red-light fantasy.

But now she was all business. Okay, he deserved her laconic attitude. He had had all day to let her know she meant something to him, but he had been strictly hands-off. Life, after all, was a series of choices.

Can't have both Good & Plenty.

Even so, after his fiery fantasies, reality was a cold bath. A low-throttled rumbling distracted him. He glanced to his right. In the next lane, sitting on a massive black-and-chrome Harley that looked as though it had been constructed from the remains of Darth Vader, sat Raven. The skull's eyes bulged grotesquely on his T-shirt. The empty sockets contrasted dramatically with the glittering slits that were formerly Raven's eyes.

"You gonna die," he said, pointing a sausage-size index finger at Russell.

He wanted to scream "Let's get the hell out of here," but his mouth refused to work. Instead, he dug his fingers into Liz's waist, hoping she would understand it as a signal to *move. Now.*

"Hey!" She flicked an angry glance over her shoulder. "Let's get a grip back there—and I don't mean that kind of grip."

Russell dipped his head to the side several times.

"Got a kink in your neck?"

He forced his lips to shape words. "Other lane."

She flashed him a perplexed look. "Lois Lane?"

"Other lane," he repeated, enunciating each word carefully in a croaky voice. He dipped his head again.

Behind them, a horn blared. An irate driver yelled, "Hey, Harley Babe. Light's green."

Liz looked over Russell's shoulder and glared at the driver. "I'm not color-blind, Datsun Dude."

Wonderful, Russell thought, trying to avoid looking at Liz as she played stare-down with Datsun Dude. He didn't want to further stir her wrath. Nor did he want to chance a glance at Brother Death in the next lane. As an alternative, he focused all his attention on a billboard that advertised an upcoming movie starring Sylvester Stallone, whose chiseled, shaved chest looked like two oversize muffins.

Surrounded by Harleys, Brother Death and the Stallone Bakery, Russell yearned for the ordinary life. The simple Honda-man life. Those earlier burning-a-path-through-life imaginings must have been from oxygen overload. A danger for the motorcycle set, no doubt.

Datsun Dude stopped his stream of irate mutterings. Liz, obviously the victor in the highway stare-down, started to turn back around when she spied Raven in the next lane.

"Go home," she said crossly, not missing a beat.

Russell swallowed hard, wondering if the sinking sensation he felt was what most men experienced before they died.

Raven shook his head no. The skull-and-crossbones earring swung wildly. "No way."

"Why?"

"'Cuz I'm gonna kill that teacher dude."

A horn honked. Another joined in.

Liz jutted her chin out. "Raven, stop being jealous."

"I ain't jealous. I just wanna do what's right by you."

Honk. Honk.

Liz swung sideways and yelled, "Datsun Dude, cool it!"

"It's not me," answered a man in a meek voice. Obviously he didn't want to tangle with Brother Death, either. "It's the guy in the Acura. Behind that...big guy on the...cycle."

Behind Raven, the driver in the cream-colored Acura rolled down his window. "Excuse me," he called out in a snotty tone, "but the light's green and you three are causing a traffic bottleneck."

Three? Wonderful. Just because he was sitting behind Liz—a prisoner of her traffic antics—he was now pegged a troublemaker.

Raven, fury blackening his face, jumped off his bike, kicked the stand and stomped back to the Acura, whose window was rolling up faster than an express elevator.

Liz, taking advantage of the moment, slammed her foot on the accelerator. Russell's head snapped back. Her Harley plunged forward, spun sideways, skidded a few feet, then straightened out. Someone screamed, the sound fading as Liz, her foot pressed on the gas, steered the Harley at lightning speed down the street.

Several blurry blocks later, Russell's wits caught up with his mind. As they eased to a stop sign, Russell thought of a quote from Thoreau: "The swiftest traveler is he that goes afoot."

Huffing breaths, Russell said, "I'll get...off here." But as he started to lift one numb leg, her Harley again bolted forward.

"I can beat him—don't sweat it!" she yelled into the wind.

He hung on to her, wishing he wasn't in this Harley–Ben Hur chariot race down the middle of Hollywood Boulevard. Behind him, he heard the ominous rumbling of Brother Death's motorcycle.

Russell leaned his forehead against the back of Liz's hair. Her silky, soft hair. Tendrils coiled wildly in the air, winding around his face.

This is the end, Russell thought. *I'm racing death, literally. My only hope is that Liz has more gas than Raven.*

Liz's Harley slowed.

Russell prayed this was just another stoplight and not an empty gas tank. He felt the cycle slow to a stop. The engine idled. Close behind, he heard the roar of Brother Death's engine.

"Liz?" he said.

"Yes?"

"I'm going to die."

"No, not today."

Russell opened his eyes. It was just a stoplight. He eased out a breath. There was hope. The light would turn green any moment and they could still outrace Brother Death...

Another sound—like a faraway screech—distracted him. He turned to his left.

In the next lane, sitting in the driver's seat of a glossy black BMW, sat Charlotte. Linking gazes with Russell, she screamed again. At least he was fairly certain it was a scream. The expensive car's engineering, plush leather interior and state-of-the-art air-conditioning absorbed such noises. It was one of the perks of being rich. You could drive in a car that muted your screams.

He offered a small smile. But Charlotte didn't see it. She was now glaring aghast at Liz, who continued to stare straight ahead, oblivious to the new drama developing in this Ben Hur remake.

Charlotte's gaze jerked to Russell's chest. She frowned, her lips moving as she read "Bop Until You Drop." Her blond hair was jiggling slightly. Either she was trembling with anger or she had the air conditioner on kill.

Russell hoped it was the air conditioner.

On his right, a motorcycle roared to a stop.

Between Sister Scream and Brother Death. *This is the story of my life,* Russell thought, his stomach descending to somewhere around his feet.

The light turned green.

This time he held his head stiff so it wouldn't snap back as Liz Knievel squealed back into the race. In his peripheral vision, he caught the sinister chrome-and-black image of Raven's bike on one side and Charlotte's shiny black BMW on the other.

And here I am seated on a Harley decorated with roses and vines.

He hoped the last picture of him would be his lying in a pool of blood on the concrete. And not across Liz's bike. Even if the T-shirt's logo was embarrassing, a sidewalk was macho. More macho than a white motorcycle decorated with petals and blossoms.

Squeezing his eyes shut, he saw the final photo of Russell Harrington. Sprawled, faceup, across a girlie Harley, his blood trickling over a background of fuchsia and crimson flowers stenciled prettily on a creamy gas tank.

He opened his eyes in time to see the BMW nose into

their lane. Like a big black shark moving in on its prey. His Raven-fantasy-death thoughts were replaced by Charlotte-fantasy-death thoughts.

Killed by a BMW driven by a deranged socialite. The ultimate nineties yuppie death.

Hunkering down a little, he peered through the passenger's window. Charlotte, her finely chiseled features sharpened with an abnormal intensity, jerked the wheel to the right, cutting off Liz's Harley.

For a brief moment, eternity suspended itself.

In that instant of time, a final regret zapped through Russell's brain. *I never made love to Liz.*

Reality returned with a swirl of movement, smell and sounds.

He watched Liz's small hands twist hard on the handlebar. Squealing tires. The stench of burning rubber. A blurred world of sky, cars and asphalt.

The bike stopped with a shriek. Or something shrieked, anyway. He hoped it wasn't him.

An awe-filled silence followed. The whoosh of traffic filled the background.

He found himself staring at the fender of Charlotte's BMW. It took a second to realize Liz had managed to stop her Harley mere inches from the car's bumper. Cautiously, not certain if his body still worked, Russell peeked over his shoulder. The bike must have skidded, because a thick foot-wide strip of black led to where the Harley now perched at a ninety-degree angle to the lane.

He breathed in slowly and exhaled. Okay, his lungs at least worked. Good. A cool, slick sweat dotted his brow. His fingers were frozen in a permanent death grip around Liz's waist.

She was leaning back against him, her head resting against his shoulder. She didn't move.

"Liz," he whispered.

No response.

He pried his fingers loose from her waist and ran his

hands up her slim arms. He held his breath, not wanting to think the worst.

"Liz," he whispered again.

"That's me," she answered in that Lauren Bacall voice. "And let me guess. Is that your lovely fiancée who almost made us roadkill?"

Through the back tinted window of the BMW, Russell watched Charlotte grapple with her seat belt.

"Yes, that's Char."

"She and Raven shouldn't drive while under the influence of jealousy."

They were in the middle lane. Cars behind them were lining up. Streams of traffic passed on their right and left, people gawking at the near accident.

"Rubberneckers," Liz fumed, stretching forward. Her red hair cascaded down her back like a veil of fire. Then she straightened, dragged her hand through her hair and dismounted from the bike.

Standing on the street, she massaged her neck. "You okay?" she asked, looking at Russell.

"I've been better." He swung his leg over the bike. As both his feet touched the asphalt, he expelled a gust of air. "Terra firma," he breathed, stepping in place. "I've never desired you as much as this moment."

"I can't believe you're making a pass at a time like this," murmured Liz.

"I was talking about terra... Never mind."

Liz wasn't listening. She struck the kickstand with her foot and glared at Charlotte.

Who, still dressed in her Aphrodite gown, emerged like angry froth from the driver's side of the BMW. She slammed the door shut and stormed toward them. A loud ripping sound followed.

She stopped abruptly, her back stiff.

"My gown," she said tersely, "is caught in the goddamn door." She glared at Russell as though he were responsible.

Even off the Harley, life continued to move too quickly.

Now he was the culprit who had ripped a gown that was at least ten feet away.

"Try opening the door," said Liz drolly, bending over to check her bike.

Charlotte's nostrils flared. She gave her skirt a yank. Another rip. She muttered a string of expletives worthy of a sailor. This wasn't the Charlotte he knew. No, this was some new creature never before seen by man. Part Aphrodite. Part Terminator.

Liz stood and crossed her arms tightly across her chest. "What the hell were you doing—trying to kill us all?"

"What the hell was *I* doing?" said Charlotte the Terminator. She crossed her arms, as well. "What the hell were *you* doing?" she accused, her face white with rage.

"Driving down the street," Liz responded, her voice as cool as Charlotte's was hot. "Let's exchange insurance information and get out of traffic."

Charlotte, used to doing what she wanted when she wanted, ignored Liz and stepped around the car until she stood in full view of Russell.

"What are you doing on the back of that...that—" she cast a withering glance in Liz's direction "—heathen's motorcycle?" She tapped her designer shoe on the dirty asphalt. She seemed to not notice the passing cars, staring eyes, honking horns. Some man had pulled his Chevy truck over to the curb and was jogging his way through the slowed traffic toward them.

"Anybody hurt?" he yelled.

But Charlotte and Liz were caught in some time-warp stare-down, similar to Liz and the Datsun Dude. Russell, not wanting to be part of this midtraffic tableau, said, "No, we're fine. Thank you."

The guy stopped next to Russell. Panting, he asked, "Are they...okay?"

"They're fine."

The guy frowned and swiped his brow. "They aren't moving."

"I'm counting my blessings."

"Are they...in shock?"

I should be so lucky. "No, they're...reenacting a scene from *High Noon.*" Drake would be proud of his movie reference.

"They're actresses?" the guy asked, his voice rising. "Rehearsing in the middle of Hollywood Boulevard?"

"Would you believe this is a publicity stunt?"

The guy squinted. "No. I think you three are a bunch of nuts. I'm gonna call the cops before somebody gets hurt."

Wonderful. A do-gooder. Just what this traumatic, dramatic life episode needed.

"Please don't. I'll get them to move their vehicles." Russell stepped closer to Mr. Do-Gooder. "Man to man," he began, clapping the stranger on the back, stealing Mr. Maday's good-ol'-boy back-clapping gimmick. "I'm having women trouble," he confessed, doing his best imitation of Mel Gibson. Or was it Harrison Ford?

The man looked at Charlotte, then Liz. "These broads mean business. What are they—ex-wives?"

A horn honked. "Get outta the road!" someone yelled, flashing a one-fingered salute.

Charlotte and Liz didn't flinch.

"They're both...fiancées," answered Russell.

The man blinked rapidly, then nodded. "You got problems, man—that's for sure." He looked at the congested traffic trying to maneuver around the BMW, Harley and stare-down. "But you're in the middle of a major street. Better move your cars—and your fiancées—before somebody gets hurt." He started to jog back through the slow-moving mass of cars. Looking back over his shoulder at Russell, he gave his head a disbelieving shake.

"Girls," Russell said loudly, walking toward them, "let's stop this nonsense and get out of here before we all end up in jail. Or the morgue."

"You haven't answered me," prodded Charlotte, tears brimming in her eyes as she looked at him.

"What?" asked Russell, waving on another driver who offered his cellular phone out the driver's window.

Charlotte's bottom lip protruded. "Russell, why were you on the back of *her* motorcycle?"

Liz stamped her foot on the ground. "I'm tired of being a third-person reference. First 'heathen.' Now 'her.' Damn it. My gold-plated calipers are scratched." She walked straight up to Charlotte and placed one red-manicured fingernail on Charlotte's Aphrodite gown. "Give me your insurance information. Now."

Honk. Honk.

Despite the situation, Russell was impressed by Liz. Her mechanical and literary sides were a sexy mix.

"Who are you?" asked Charlotte in that half pouty, half enraged voice that Russell knew too well.

Russell stepped forward. Forget the calipers. Something else would be scratched—his eyeballs—if Liz spilled her name. But just as Russell opened his mouth to say something, *anything,* a menacing rumble vibrated through the air.

Raven eased his Darth Vader Harley next to Liz's. His face was darker than the black beast he rode. Seeing Russell, he raised his upper lip in a sneer that creased one whole side of his face. He slammed his foot against the stand and cut the ignition.

"Lizzy," he barked. "You okay?"

Months later, Russell would still have difficulty recalling the exact sequence of events.

"Lizzy?" repeated Charlotte, frowning. Her mouth dropped open. "Liz!" she squealed in a pitch reserved for singing the national anthem. She ran in place, as though unsure what to do, then made a beeline for Russell.

Liz, obviously stunned by the Aphrodite-Terminator's reaction, threw herself across her bike. Later she told Russell that she thought Charlotte was going to attack it.

Raven, never one who lived fully in the here and now, stood stone-still, his mouth opened wide as if for a dental checkup.

Charlotte, upon reaching Russell, raised her hands—

clawlike—into the air, then grabbed the Bop Until You Drop T-shirt.

Another loud, prolonged rip.

Russell looked down. His T-shirt was shredded in two, exposing his chest. This was becoming a bad habit, having his clothes removed forcibly in public.

"Liz!" Charlotte screeched again, pointing a pink-frosted fingertip at Russell's chest. She swiveled like some kind of deranged robot and stopped when her pointing finger landed on Liz.

"You!" said Charlotte, her finger frozen midpoint. "You're *Liz*."

In the following moments of awkward silence, Russell checked out Charlotte's backside. When she had yanked her dress out of the door, she had ripped out a panel of her gown.

The panel that covered her rear end.

"Charlotte," said Russell quietly, staring at her sheer silk panties.

"Don't talk to me," she answered angrily, still pointing at Liz.

"Your gown—"

"You're obstructing traffic," a gruff voice interrupted. "Is anyone hurt?"

Russell shifted his gaze to the left. There stood a police officer, his face grim. His officer buddy was waving traffic around the *High Noon* reenactment. Another unit eased to stop behind them and turned on its flashing lights.

"Why is your name on my fiancé's chest?" Charlotte cried out, waving her finger like a loaded gun.

"Charlotte…" Russell began. The police officer had glanced down at her backside, then at Russell's ripped T-shirt. *Naked in Hollywood*. That would be the title of his autobiography—if he lived to write it.

"Shut up, Russell," Charlotte warned.

"Ma'am," the officer said, approaching her from behind. He gently touched her on the shoulder. "Ma'am."

She pivoted, her arm stuck in accusing-finger-pointing

mode. Halfway through her turn, her hand slammed into the officer's side.

The officer caught her arm. "That's enough, now. Are you hurt?"

She grabbed the officer's arm. "Let go of me, you oaf!" She swung back one designer-shoe foot and planted a neat kick in the officer's shin.

Pandemonium broke loose.

Two other officers ran into the middle of the group. One grabbed Charlotte's arms and bent them behind her back. Handcuffs were clamped on her faster than you could say "There's a sale at Neiman's."

"My fiancé has another woman's name on his chest," Charlotte wailed, seeming more upset over the tattoo than the fact that she was seminaked and shackled.

Another officer was hovering over Liz, who was still spread-eagled over her motorcycle.

Raven, his eyes wide with hurt, suddenly came to life. "Hey, dudes, that's a lady!" He stormed toward Charlotte.

Seeing the monster-size man with Brother Death on his T-shirt hurtling across the asphalt, a fourth officer yelled, "Hold it there, buddy! Halt!"

Traffic was at a dead stop. One man, chewing gum, asked Russell, "Hey, what show are they shooting?"

Russell glanced over his shoulder. "Brother Death, if he's not careful."

The man made a bubble and snapped it.

Raven fell to the ground, obviously thinking he had been shot.

Liz screamed.

Two more officers ran toward Raven, their guns pulled.

Charlotte continued to scuffle with the two officers, her rear end flashing more pink and white than Liz's Harley.

Bright lights. Clattering sounds.

Russell's spirits hit bottom. There was a TV crew, taking pictures of the melee. When the lights flashed in his direction, he looked away. But not before he saw Charlotte's behind photographed for all posterity.

An officer was at his side. "Are you all right?"

"Physically? Yes," answered Russell.

"Are you the driver of one of these vehicles?"

"No, I was a passenger. On that Harley over there."

"The big black one?"

"No, the pink-and-white one."

"Do you know these other people?"

"Yes." *Unfortunately.*

"The woman?" The officer nodded toward Charlotte, who was now facing the cameras, her face contorted as she spewed more sailorisms.

"Yes. She's my fiancée."

The officer frowned. "I thought that other woman..."

Russell sighed audibly. "Yes, she's my fiancée, too."

The officer gave his head a shake, although Russell was certain he caught a twinkle in the man's eyes. "Why don't you and fiancée number two leave. We have enough to take care of here."

Russell felt as though he'd swallowed a tray of ice cubes. Raven was being handcuffed and led away. Charlotte was being neatly stuffed into the back seat of a police car. Liz was sitting astride her Harley, checking some apparatus. Probably her calipers, whatever they were.

"Thank you, Officer...Officer Kl-Klenck..." Russell squinted and tried to decipher the name on the badge.

"Don't try to pronounce it. I might have to arrest you for insulting an officer." One corner of his mouth twisted upward.

Charlotte was in handcuffs. Raven was the new SWAT team poster boy. And in the midst of this insanity, a police officer was making arrest jokes. Only in L.A.

Deciding not to chance further conversation, Russell nodded and started to walk away.

"Uh, before you go," said the policeman.

Russell looked over his shoulder.

"Sometimes two isn't better than one."

Russell released a pent-up breath, nodded, then continued walking toward Liz's Harley.

"You're telling me," he muttered.

9

SITTING ASTRIDE her Harley, Liz turned the ignition key. A dark-eyed cop, with a shiny gold name tag that read D. Klencke, had told her she was free to leave. She pumped the gas pedal and glanced around. There were more lights, people and commotion here than in the carnival when she was a kid. Except instead of the aroma of popcorn and cotton candy, this place reeked of exhaust and flares.

Through the haze of smoke and police, she searched for Russell. With all these black cop uniforms, a white T with Bop Until You Drop in purple lettering should be easy to pick out. She frowned, remembering Charlotte's war cry followed by a ripping sound. Even though Liz had been spread-eagled across her bike, she had had zero doubt what was being ripped.

Well, even half a T, with a Bop or a Drop, would be a cinch to find. She craned her neck and looked through another mass of uniformed bodies.

No Russell.

Poor guy. With his luck, he was probably handcuffed to Ms Bel Air. Liz pressed her lips together. Served him right. Being cuffed would be good practice for a marriage where they'd be chained together for life.

She started to turn the handlebar when something caught the corner of her eye. She turned. Against a background of black shirts emerged a trim, naked torso. Russell's naked torso. Bop Until You Drop was history.

She fought the urge to smile. *That Charlotte has some grip.*

Liz felt like humming "Unchained Melody" but instead

called out, "Over here, Russ." As he headed her way, she decided to kick back and enjoy the view.

He had a loose-hipped walk, the kind she liked on a guy. It stated an easygoing confidence. Amazingly, his pants were wrinkle-free despite their wild ride and near accident. Her gaze rose to his head. Couldn't say the same for his hair—it had reverted to the "wind-tunnel" look.

Neat pants and wild hair.

Half Russell, half Max.

She dropped her gaze. His deliciously naked chest was lean, but it had some well-proportioned bulk in his shoulders and upper arms. She squeezed the handlebar. Not too much meat—just enough to hold on to.

I wouldn't do a death grip like Charlotte, Liz promised herself. *I'd give you room to be yourself. To write your action-adventure screenplays. To be "Max." To wear any ol' T-shirt you damn well pleased.*

Closer now, she could clearly see the tat. Across a red heart that rested on his own, she read her name. *Liz.*

Where it belongs. She blinked back a surge of emotion. He was only a few feet away—close enough to catch any tell-tale thoughts on her face. She lowered her head and stared at the instrument panel, pretending to be preoccupied with something.

"Sometimes two isn't better than one," he said when he reached her. "Let's leave this den of iniquity." He dragged a hand through his hair, wincing when his fingers got stuck in the mass. "Good Lord. The hair from hell is back."

She looked up. "I like it. Draws attention to you."

"And I thought everyone was staring at me because of my sculpted chest."

"That, too." Heat filled her cheeks. Damn, she had wanted to play it cool and here she was blushing like a smitten teenager. "So what happened to the T?" she asked, trying to sound nonchalant.

"Charlotte sharpened her nails on it."

Liz bit her tongue so as not to say "Maybe you should

get her a scratching post." Her inflamed cheeks already said too much.

She thumped the seat behind her. "Hop on."

He hitched one leg over the back of the Harley with a familiarity that gave her heart a twist. No guy had spent as much time on her bike as Russell these past few days. Or as much time in her thoughts.

Or her heart.

"Let's blow this joint," he said, gripping her waist.

She looked around, trying to concentrate on how best to exit, but all she could think about was how the heat of his hands burned through her clothes. And how close that naked chest was to her.

She liked how his hands spanned her waist. They were large hands. A writer's hands. He was probably very good with them, no matter what he was doing...

Life would be much simpler when Russell Harrington was married and gone from her life.

She eased down on the gas pedal and pulled forward. Steering the bike around a flare, she caught an image of Raven being escorted to a police car. She jerked to a stop and watched as the big black bulk was carted toward a squad car by four officers. "They nabbed Raven, too. What'd he do?"

"After being shot by Bubble Gum, he attempted to single-handedly save Aphrodite-Terminator's life."

Liz looked over her shoulder at Russell. "Have you been in an alternative universe?"

He cocked one eyebrow. "Are you stealing my lines?"

I'd like to steal your heart. She forced the thought out of her head and returned to the conversation. "Bubble Gum? Terminator?"

"Raven kissed the asphalt after someone popped their gum. Then, when he saw Charlotte being handcuffed, he raced to her defense. Unfortunately, one doesn't attempt such heroic acts when the police are yelling things like 'Hold it there, buddy' and 'Halt.'"

"Raven was probably caught in one of his time warps."

"Well, he's now caught by the LAPD."

Liz rolled her shoulders and breathed out slowly. Even though she prided herself on managing crises well, this Hollywood Boulevard near catastrophe had jarred her nerves big time. "Hang on," she said softly before pulling out into traffic.

Several minutes later, she stopped at a red light.

Russell leaned forward and rested his chin on her shoulder. "You all right?" he asked. "That was some fiasco we just barely survived."

"Fine," she answered. Which was a half-truth. Her body had survived the near accident. But she doubted if her mind and heart would survive Russell Harrington. "Shall I take the 10 to Santa Monica?"

"Good Lord, no. After what we've been through, I'd prefer not to fly down an L.A. freeway on this machine. Cut to Olympic. Or Pico. We'll take the scenic route."

She laughed. "Scenic, huh?"

He rubbed one of her bare arms. Spasms of electricity rippled over her skin.

"After the scene we just created," he said, sounding oblivious to her reaction, "a string of run-down apartment buildings and decaying palm trees is about all the *scenic* I can handle."

Thirty minutes later, she pulled up in front of his apartment building. The outside was nothing to write home about—her Hollywood apartment had a lot more character. Russell's building looked like a square pumpkin. Flat orange walls with square windows for eyes and nose. In front, a nothing strip of lawn. Not even wide enough to sunbathe on. But Santa Monica was prime apartment space. Would-be renters waited months to set down roots in such pumpkin patches.

She cut the engine and slipped off the bike. The sun was settling low. Wisps of pink-and-gold clouds streaked the sky. The sweet scent of honeysuckle laced the air.

Russell stood next to her. "Home sweet home," he said, gesturing to the building. His arm dropped. "Damn."

"What?"

"My keys."

"What about them?"

"They were in my T. The first one, not the second. The one Raven repossessed back at your place."

"You're saying your keys are back in Hollywood?" she asked slowly.

"Yes, but I still have your coin purse!" He pulled it out of his pocket, smiling. His grin faded as he saw her reaction. "Well, let's get back on your bike—"

"No way. You're talking to a girl who has many talents—one of which is breaking into locked apartments. Locked tattoo parlors. Locked anything." She flashed him a grin. "All I need is a hairpin. I probably have one in my bike's travel compartment—let me check."

She snatched the coin purse from Russell on her way back to her bike. Once there, she flipped open a side panel, tossed her coin purse inside and began rummaging through the panel's other contents. A few moments later, she whirled around and lifted a hairpin for his inspection. "Be Prepared—that's my motto."

"Now you're stealing lines from the Boy Scouts." He perused her bike. "That Dream Girl is some feminine Harley. What else do you have in it—a sewing machine?"

"Feminine? Because I like pink and carry a few hairpins, you think I can't talk shop?" She huffed indignantly and leveled him a look. "I bought it stock so I could customize it. I massaged more power into this baby by notching the pistons, cutting the valves, adding titanium springs, porting and flowing the heads and installing a special cam and ignition. After that, the horsepower hit about sixty-eight on the dyno giving it a top speed of one thirty-five." She paused, waiting for his reaction. "Bet you didn't do that with your Honda."

"If I told you I got new brake pads, would you be impressed?"

"'Nuff said," she answered, turning the hairpin in her

palm. "We'll be inside before you can say 'Aren't those pants too tight.'"

She headed toward the stairs, pleased she had scored some points with her bike talk. Guys were like that—didn't think a girl knew a piston from a pot holder. A mischievous part of her wanted to score a few more points. Give him something to remember. After all, they'd never see each other after today.

Halfway up the walk to his building, she stopped. Jutting out one hip, she swiveled a little and shot him a glance over her shoulder.

Sure enough. He was staring at her bottom line.

"Checking out Yeats's symbolism again?"

"Hmmm?" He jerked his head up. "Uh, no. Thinking about D.H. Lawrence."

"Next you'll tell me an excerpt from *Women in Love* is on my—" She winked.

She continued up the walk, pleased with her effect. It was a small perk, but a much-needed one for her ego. Charlotte might have him for the rest of her life, but Liz had had his undivided attention—or imagination—for a few heated moments back there.

His apartment was at the top of the first stair landing. She remembered the type of knob—seemed most places had a variation of these round jobbies. This was a cinch. She could pick it in her sleep. After unbending the hairpin, she needed only a few seconds to click the door open.

"Home sweet home," she said, motioning to Russell to come inside.

"Unbelievable," he murmured, walking past her. "Where'd you learn that trick?"

"My dad. A master of many talents. Too bad he never believed in himself." She followed him inside.

Russell shut the door. "What's that supposed to mean?"

"He never believed in his dreams. Remember? I swore I'd never be like that." She looked around, avoiding his stare. "This place is wall-to-wall books. What'd you do? Hold up a librarian?"

Chuckling, Russell flicked a switch on the wall. In the corner, a standing lamp lighted, permeating the room with a warm glow. "I began acquiring books at a young age, thanks to my dad."

"Lucky you. He encouraged your dreams."

"He encouraged everybody's dreams," Russell snapped. He took a breath and closed his eyes. "Sorry. You hit a button. You see, my dad's profession was 'dreamer.' Family, groceries, bills came in second. Or third or fourth." He made a waving motion. "Somewhere down the list, anyway. I swore I'd never be like that."

He threaded his fingers together and stretched them over his head. "It's been a harrowing few hours. Need to...freshen up?"

"I'm okay."

"I'll only be a minute. Then I need to call the LAPD and figure out how to track down my vigilante fiancée."

He cut Liz a glance. But before she could decipher what it meant, he had exited the room.

"I would have loved Dad to encourage my dreams," she murmured. A silver-framed picture, strategically placed on top of a small bookshelf, caught her eye. She crossed the room to get a closer look.

A family photo. The father, dressed in a checkered shirt and slacks, stood protectively over his brood. Even in this photo, you could see the twinkle in his eyes. The same twinkle she'd seen in Russell's when he was about to say something amusing.

Seated in the center, holding a baby, had to be the mother. Her softly rounded face looked at the camera with such sweetness that it made Liz's insides ache. Her own mother had died when Liz was five—her hazy memories consisted of a pretty, lively woman with long red hair and a wide smile.

She gazed intently at the woman. Her gaze shifted to the right. Standing next to his mother were two kids, a boy and a girl. She leaned closer and scrutinized the picture. The gray-eyed boy had neatly parted sandy brown hair. The same hairstyle she remembered Russell wore that first night. Well, before the bike ride, anyway.

She tilted her head. What was wrong with this picture? Then she realized: he stared into the lens with a strange smile. As though he were hiding something. Braces? Liz cupped her hand to her mouth so as to not laugh out loud. Well, of course. Teenage Russell Harrington didn't want to flash his metal teeth.

Her smile faded as she shifted her gaze back to the father in the photograph. Gently touching the glass over the man's face, she remembered Russell's words. *My dad's profession was 'dreamer.' Family, groceries, bills came in second. Or third...*

She straightened and turned around, not wanting to be caught snooping. Fighting down a swell of guilt, she quickly crossed to the couch and sat down. Then popped back up. She felt too antsy to sit still. Her mind was still tumbling with their conversation about dads and dreams.

Her dad had refused to dream, whereas Russell's dad was the exact opposite. That certainly explained a few things. For one, why Russell acted so defensively when they talked about dreams. And why "Max" didn't pursue his own dream of writing action-adventure screenplays.

It also explained why he would settle down with a predictable, conventional woman. With a rush of understanding, she suddenly knew why Russell, no matter what he might feel for her, would still marry Charlotte. *Predictable Charlotte means a life free of dreams. Free of failures.*

Liz stared absently at the drapes on the front windows. The textured beige fabric hung in smooth, linear lines. The same fabric covered the tasseled throw pillows on the couch. Instinctively, Liz knew this wasn't Russell's taste. Undoubtedly these were the touch of Charlotte.

Charlotte's touch.

Does Russell react to her touch as he does to mine?

Liz swallowed hard, suddenly feeling an overwhelming ache in her heart. She and Russell fitted together. Like the way they fitted together on her bike. They loved books, writing, they shared a sense of humor and passionate natures—not that they'd had much of a chance to express it, or act on it with each other.

A sting of tears threatened the corners of her eyes. Aimlessly, she walked around the living room, ending up at the chair positioned next to the couch. She made a fist and sank it against the back of the chair. Damn it. She'd been around the block enough times to recognize the real thing.

What we have is real, Russell. It's not beige and acceptable. It's multicolored and desirable. It's life and joy and passion and...dreams.

No, that's the one thing they didn't share. Her insides caved in. She couldn't be with a man who didn't dream. She bit her lip. Be with? As though that were an option. He was already spoken for, dreamer or no dreamer.

"I don't know where to start," Russell said, coming back into the room.

She swiped at her eye and pretended to find the corduroy covering of the chair fascinating. "Start?"

"There must be dozens of police stations in Los Angeles. How do I know which lucky precinct is the new quarters of Charlotte Maday, the skirtless wonder."

Liz looked up. "At least you're no longer the shirtless wonder," she quipped, hoping he didn't hear the quaver in her voice. He had thrown on a long-sleeved white shirt but hadn't buttoned it. A corner of the tat could be seen. Half a heart and the letter *L.*

"Maybe I'll call 911," Russell continued, "and ask if they've seen Charlotte Maday and her new priest-turned-bodyguard, Brother Death."

"That might work," agreed Liz. She smiled, but it felt tight, unreal. She clutched the back of the chair. *Hold on. Shift gears. You can make it through.* "Check the white pages under City Government," she suggested. "There must be a listing of stations. While you're at it, I'll call Auntie and make sure she's not doing tats in my absence. Where's your phone?"

"In the dining room, off the kitchen." He pointed behind

him to a small butcher-block table with two matching
wooden seats. Mounted on the wall was a beige phone.
"Auntie doing tats? You mean some poor man will wake
up tomorrow morning with 'Auntie' engraved on his
chest?"

"Don't mess with me," said Liz, sashaying past, wondering if Charlotte had also picked out the color of the
telephone. As though she wanted to bleach all the color—
all the passion—out of his life. "Or I'll add more to your
tat."

"Like what? Your social security number?"

She picked up the receiver and punched in the number
of The Rose Tattoo. "Very funny."

"Remind Charlotte how funny I am when she attempts
to remove the tattoo with her fingernails."

"Attempts? She did a pretty thorough job on your
T-shirt."

"She does a pretty good job at most things. Because
she's a *Maday*."

A shadow crossed Liz's face.

"Did I say something wrong…?"

But she turned away, engrossed in making her call.

Russell absently scraped his knuckles against his chin,
pondering the emotion that had flashed in her green eyes.
She had looked…*sad*. Even now, staring at Liz's back, he
was aware of the slump of her shoulders, as though a sor-
row burdened her.

Surely she didn't care what Charlotte did to the tattoo.

Or did she?

Bam, bam, bam.

He flinched. Clutching his chest, he cautiously looked
down at his fresh shirt, half expecting to see bleeding bullet
holes.

Bam, bam.

He jerked his gaze to the front door. Hardly gunfire—it
was just loud knocking. He stealthily crossed into the dining room and stood behind Liz, glad she hadn't witnessed
his faux-death experience.

"I thought Brother Death was on a field trip to jail," he whispered loudly.

Bam, bam.

Shifting the receiver to her other ear, Liz looked up into Russell's face. "What do you think I have? An antenna hookup in my brain to the LAPD? How should I know where Raven is—" She held up one hand to stop the conversation.

"Auntie?" she said sweetly into the receiver. "Hold on one minute." She cupped one hand over the mouthpiece. "Answer the door. Nothing terrible can happen."

"You're one to talk."

She waved Russell away and turned back to her conversation. "Auntie? I have something to tell you..."

Russell frowned. Great. She was leaving him to play butler to Brother Death. He approached the door.

Bam, bam.

Why did the cretin even bother knocking? Why not blast the door open with one blow of his hairy chicken fist?

Gripping the doorknob, Russell inhaled deeply before speaking. "Who is it?" he said in his best macho voice.

"Who am I?" Drake said, his voice muffled. "Who are you? Charles Bronson?"

Russell pulled open the door. "Everybody's a comic these days."

Looking at Russell's hair, Drake did a dramatic double take. "Yowza, buddy. When did you get the Lyle Lovett do?"

Russell just gave Drake a scornful look, ignoring his comment. Drake dropped his hands and strolled in. "And since when do you ask who's at the door?"

"Since my life began resembling a wacko biker flick."

Drake laughed, then looked Russell up and down. "Seriously, buddy. You okay?"

"I never know these days. I just wing it from moment to moment." Russell shut the door, wondering how Drake always looked so put together. Today he had on a blue short-sleeved pullover and neatly creased linen pants. "Tell me—what's it like to wear nice, clean, pressed clothes that someone isn't trying to rip off your body?''

"Who says I don't want them ripped off? A man's gotta dream." Drake cocked his head. "Speaking of dreaming, I hear a female voice. And it's not your garden blue-blood variety."

"Plenty's here. I'm surprised you didn't recognize the rose-stenciled Harley with the beaded leather fringes out front."

"Hadn't seen it in the light before. Thought Biker Barbie had moved into the neighborhood." Drake craned his head to catch a look of Liz. He emitted a low whistle. "What I'd give to be Ken. Tell me I haven't died and gone to heaven."

"You haven't. But I wish I had. Much preferable to the last few days when I have personally descended into Dante's hell. The last level, I fear, will be seen on tonight's news—"

"Will be? You and your cast of characters already starred on Channel nine's early telecast." He lowered his voice. "Charlotte, by the way, makes quite a backup singer"—he wiggled his eyebrows—"if you get my drift."

Russell sighed heavily. "Charlotte doesn't even like to be seen in a bathing suit. Now all the world knows what her underwear looks like."

"And more," confided Drake. "Those were pretty sheer undies."

"French silk."

"Ooo-la-la. According to the reporter, Charlotte the very Good has been very, very naughty."

"They showed footage of her being handcuffed?" When Drake nodded, Russell groaned. "And the Madays thought *my* picture was bad."

"The reporter said she'd fired a gun at some priest by the name of Brother...Brother..."

"Death."

Drake placed a comforting hand on Russell's back. "Lighten up, buddy. Try to focus on living."

Russell backed up and flopped into a chair.

Drake glanced at Liz, then back to Russell. He turned his back to Liz and whispered, "What kind of power do you have over women, anyway?" He lowered his gaze to Russell's chest. "The secret is in the tattoo. Ever since you got that thing, you've become the next Warren Beatty. I want one. Today. Now. This very minute."

"Get a handle on it. We're in the middle of a crisis here."

In the ensuing silence, fragments of Liz's conversation could be overheard. "She's not a nudist...her dress ripped. That's why her butt, I mean behind, was exposed..."

Drake scratched his chin and stared up at the ceiling. "I wonder when Charlotte will find out her secrets have been bared."

"Who cares about when," Russell said. "What's frightening is *what* she'll do. There is no fury like a woman unadorned."

Drake smiled gleefully as he dropped his gaze back to Russell.

"Boy, you've had it rough, buddy. Can I get you something? A little Wild Turkey to smooth the rough edges?" Drake asked.

"On the rocks. Make it a double."

As Drake went into the kitchen, Liz hung up the phone and headed back into the living room. She stopped next to Russell's chair and stood there expectantly.

The soft evening light illuminated the beige drapes with a dreamy glow. Against this luminous backdrop, Liz's shapely form was outlined. He started to speak, but his tongue refused to cooperate. All he could do was stare at her Pre-Raphaelite hair, tapered waist, slightly rounded hips. His fingers twitched as he imagined his hands hugging those hips...

A memory flared through his mind. Sitting here in a chair with Liz standing in front of him was reminiscent of that first morning in her tattoo parlor. She had helped him unbutton his shirt, then touched the edges of the tattoo, the heat of her hands igniting small fires across his skin.

He breathed in sharply and clutched his chest.

"You okay, Max?"

That husky Lauren Bacall voice. Calling him Max.

His secret name. The name attached to his dreams.

"I like it when you call me Max," he confessed.

"Max," Drake repeated loudly, entering the room. With a flourish, he handed the Wild Turkey to Russell. "And I like it when you call me irresponsible."

"Which, by the way," Russell said, accepting the drink, "you were when you left the name of the restaurant on Liz's phone machine."

Drake frowned. "I don't get it."

"Raven overheard it and made a beeline to Chez Nous. The ensuing restaurant scene made the Madays' pool party look like a picnic." He took a sip, relishing the sting of bourbon. "Of course, the Hollywood Boulevard scene made the restaurant scene look like a segment of *The Waltons.*" He took another sip. "If this continues, the next scene should be nominated for an Academy Award."

"Best Dramatic Confrontation?" offered Drake.

"Something like that," Russell said, setting the drink on a side table. "I've been avoiding this moment, but I need to begin calling police stations and see if a Charlotte Maday has checked in." He started to stand.

"No need to," Liz said. "Auntie saw the news and informed me that both Charlotte and Raven have been released. Seems the D.A.'s office isn't pressing charges against Charlotte. Something about kicking not resulting in bodily injury. Raven, however, has a court date for 'obstruction.' After the other antics Auntie's witnessed, it didn't throw her too much to see everyone on the news cavorting in the middle of Hollywood Boulevard—although she expressed concern that I'd want to marry into that."

"Of course you don't want to marry into *that,*" said Russell defensively, sitting straighter.

A faint pink crept up Liz's throat. "Of course not. But

I had to say I was marrying into *that* in order to get my trust fund. But that was only because I have to marry *somebody* and you were naked in my living room so I had to say I was marrying you.'' The pink deepened to red.

Drake raised his hand. ''I'm not naked, but I'm in a living room and I'm available.''

Ignoring him, Russell continued, ''What if I hadn't been naked in your living ro—'' He broke off and retrieved his drink. ''Never mind.''

''I don't even know why we're having this conversation. I don't marry men who are tagged by someone else. Besides, I'm marrying Raven.'' She lifted her chin a notch, as though to enforce her statement.

But he caught that look in her eyes again. As if she were filled with regret. For what they could have been? Was he imagining that this tempestuous beauty could actually fall for him, an English professor with Lyle Lovett hair and a shrinking closet? For an instant, he indulged the fantasy. Winning the love of Liz would be better than getting tenure, being granted eternal life and never again having a bad-hair day.

Crazy thoughts. A life with Liz would never work. He'd seen that kind of marriage before—his parents' marriage. Even as a kid, he'd learned that marriage and dreams didn't mix.

''Time for you to go, Drake.'' Russell stood abruptly and headed for the front door. ''Liz and I need to return to Hollywood, get my car.''

''I want to tell Barbie—I mean Liz—something before I go,'' Drake said. Clearing his throat, he turned to her and pressed his palm over his heart. ''If you change your mind about Raven, call me. I'd love to be engaged.''

''And I'd love to throw you a bachelor party, ' Russell said, opening the front door. ''I'll call you later.''

Drake held up both hands in truce. ''Sure thing, Max.'' He blew Liz a kiss, then headed toward the door. ''We never did discuss this Max thing, by the way.''

''And we never will,'' Russell responded firmly.

"Oh," Drake said, stopping. "Is the wedding still on? The one with you and Charlotte, I mean. After all, I'm the best man. I need to know if I should pick up the tux on Saturday." He smiled impishly at Liz. "Have you wondered if anybody ever got buried in a rented tux?"

She giggled.

Russell shot Drake a sharp look. "If someone doesn't leave now, that could happen on Saturday. Wedding or no wedding."

Drake had barely waved goodbye before Russell shut the door.

"He's sweet," said Liz, sitting on the couch.

"The adjective I usually think of is 'smooth.'" He walked back into the living room.

"If I had met him that first night instead of you, none of this would have happened."

A rush of pain filled his gut. He looked at his half-filled glass on the table, pondering if a few sips of bourbon could set his insides on fire. But the feeling wasn't contained in his gut. It also burned in his chest. Not a physical burn, more a psychic kind of pain.

I'm jealous, he realized. He had felt this earlier, and now he experienced it again. *I don't want any other man to have Liz.*

Good Lord, he'd never felt like this about Charlotte. In fact, with Charlotte, everything was tempered, planned, emotionally nondescript. Life was a series of art showings and restaurants, all punctuated by the daily Maday cocktail hour.

Then that world had shattered. In less than a week, he'd gone from socializing with the upper crust to drag racing with the Hell's Angels. From feeling contented to feeling impassioned.

He'd never felt so alive, so vital.

"Isn't that true?" Liz prompted. "None of this would have happened if I had met Drake instead of you?"

He tried to sound rational and unaffected. "My life would certainly have been simpler." No crazy emotions.

No wild escapades. After too many years in academia, he was finally *experiencing* life instead of intellectualizing it.

He chanced a look at her. She was staring back at him with the sparkling green eyes that promised more than he'd ever dared wish for. The heated memory of their shared kisses—warm, moist, needy—stirred his thoughts. Those luscious lips. A man could spend a lifetime kissing those lips.

"What are you thinking?" asked Liz.

"I'm marrying Charlotte's lips on Saturday." He scratched his temple. "I mean, I'm marrying Charlotte."

She frowned. Her full red lips pursed a little in confusion. "Isn't that called a non sequitur?"

"What?"

"You were agreeing that your life would have been simpler if we hadn't met, then you said you were marrying Charlotte's lips. Are you all right?"

He cleared his throat. "We need to go now. To Hollywood. Get keys." He let out a whoosh of breath. "Listen to me—I resort to sentence fragments when I'm around you. Because you reduce me to a primitive state." He paced several steps before pivoting and facing her squarely. "Because of you, I have lost the benefits of millions of years of evolution. I have become nothing more than a quivering, gelatinous mass of emotions and desires." He closed his eyes. "I shouldn't have said all this."

After a pause, Liz said quietly, "What you're really saying is that you like me."

He opened his eyes. "To state it bluntly, yes."

She leaned forward and put her hands on her knees. "Then I'm going to be bold and say it like it is. We're more soul mates than you'll ever be with Ms Bel Air. You and I, we could set the world on fire. But I could never encroach on another woman's man. Well, willfully. And with you, my will has crumbled, that's for sure. But I don't regret anything we've shared. In fact, I'll treasure it always."

They stared at each other for what seemed a small eter-

nity. Outside a bird twittered a solitary tune. In those moments, Russell had never yearned more for someone than
he did for Liz.

"Can I ask one favor before I go?" she finally asked,
breaking the silence.

"Anything."

"Let me see your screenplay. Let me see your dream."
He hesitated. "No one's—"

"It's cool. After today, I'll never see you again. No one
will ever know you shared it with me."

He rubbed his jaw thoughtfully, then turned and pulled
a manuscript from a bookshelf. After settling next to her
on the couch, he placed the book into her hands.

She read the title page out loud. "*NeuroWorld* by Max
Harrington. Max," she said in a husky undertone and
smiled.

That voice again. He closed his eyes, wanting to memorize how she said the name. Wanting to etch the honeyed
tenor of her words deep into his cortex, into a secret region
that he could return to over the years when he wanted to
remember Liz.

When he opened his eyes, she was avidly reading.

Fifteen minutes later, she stopped. "So far, a terrific
story!"

"You don't have to say that just because I'm sitting
here."

"You're brilliant. I can't believe all this stuff came out
of your head."

"It's bizarre, I know—"

"No!" She stood up, holding the screenplay in front of
her. "It's magical. It's…thrilling. I was enthralled with
those people, the Hed—Hed—" She flipped the book open
and scanned a page.

"Hedones," explained Russell. "Shorthand for *hedo-
nists.* Guess that succinctly explains their motivation."

"Yeah, they were pretty hot-blooded." The way she felt
now. The way Russell Harrington had been with her that
first night. She glanced down at the book and realized it

was shaking. Because she was shaking. Damn. And he thought he was the only one to be reduced to a mass of emotions? Thanks to Russell Harrington, she was turning into a pile of weak-kneed mush.

"And, uh," she began, her voice barely above a whisper. "The action was better than a Steven Seagal movie."

"Thank you. I think."

She kept her eyes lowered. "And...it freaked me out when the Aca—Aca—"

"Academions."

"Yes, them. It freaked me out when they descended from that ivory-colored ship." She looked up. His eyes twinkled with humor. Just like his dad in the photograph, she thought.

"You know, Academions. The overly educated seers who fly in that ivory-colored contraption."

"Right, they're self-centered. Full of themselves." Maybe if she kept the conversation going, he wouldn't look down and see how the book was vibrating faster than one of those flying ships.

"My feelings exactly." He reached out and took the screenplay from her trembling fingers. "Your reaction means more to me than you know."

"The shaking, really?" She rubbed her hands together. "I'd hoped you didn't notice."

Russell stood and laid a warm hand on her own. "It's okay, Millicent."

She almost heard her father's gentle tone in Russell's voice. Tears filmed her vision.

"Is that too familiar to call you by your given name?"

She started to shake her head no, but turned away instead. "Just reminded me of my dad. That's all."

"But you prefer Liz. Or Elizabeth."

"Yes."

"Must have been difficult for your father to start calling you by another name."

"It was difficult for him to believe in my dreams." Her voice broke on the word "dreams."

When Russell gently pulled her toward him, she didn't fight it. As he wrapped her in his arms, she realized how long it had been since she'd felt sheltered, protected, and she sank against him, grateful for the warmth of his embrace.

Pressed against his chest, she felt the texture of his cotton shirt against her cheek, heard the beating of his heart. The woodsy scent of his cologne coiled around her, filling her senses.

"You don't have to be strong, Liz. You can let go."

She thought about pulling away, but Russell held her close. Placing her arms around him, she held on and let the tears flow. All the while, Russell held her near, stroked her hair, murmured consoling words.

Finally, her tears stopped. Rubbing the last trace of them from her eyes, she leaned back and looked into Russell's face. "I look like a raccoon."

"I wouldn't know. I've never been face-to-face with a raccoon before."

"I should go wash my face."

"Wait a minute." He lightly wiped underneath one eye. "There. Now you look like a fawn."

"Fawn?"

"Okay, red fox."

She smiled. "Not only are you a good writer, you're a charmer, too."

"Then can I charm you into one last favor? After all, fair's fair."

"Anything."

"Kiss me. Just once. I want to remember the taste of your love."

She lowered her head slightly. "'Unless you can die when the dream is past—oh never call it loving.'"

"Elizabeth Barrett Browning."

"That's my secret dream, you know. Besides going to college and teaching and writing—to get my sonnets published."

He placed his hands on her shoulders. "I want you to

have your dreams, Liz. I just don't want to sacrifice reality for my own.''

"But you've already sacrificed," she murmured softly.

She raised her lips to his and moaned when his mouth pressed against hers. He didn't just kiss her lips, he possessed them. As his tongue penetrated her mouth, his hands roamed feverishly over her back. She arched against him, aching to feel the length of his body against hers.

"Oh, Liz," he groaned, gasping for air. He planted small kisses on her cheek, her hair, her neck. She clung to him, her breath escaping in pants. It would be so easy to take it further...to fully indulge their pent-up desires.

"I want you," he said in a low, throaty tone.

"I want you, too." She placed a single kiss on his chin and then gently, but firmly, stepped out of his arms. "Even if you were available, we wouldn't last. You're unable to trust your dreams. Been there, done that."

His eyes turned liquid. "And I couldn't live a life where dreams took priority over reality. Been there—" he reached out and stroked her hair "—done that."

He picked up the screenplay and stuck it back into the bookcase. "Thanks for the encouraging words about my story."

"You're a wonderful writer. You should submit it."

Unable to say more, she crossed to the door and exited. The balmy evening breezes were little comfort for the hurt in her heart. She stopped on the sidewalk and looked up at a single star that glittered in the twilight sky. Behind her, she heard Russell close the door with a solid click.

Inside her heart, she closed another door and silently bade him goodbye.

10

LIZ TURNED and checked her reflection in the full-length mirror. The white lace minidress cinched her waist, then fell in soft pleats to her midthigh. She remembered the day she and Auntie had shopped for the wedding gown. At first Auntie had questioned its length—"Sweetie, you'll catch cold"—but had ended up agreeing it was Liz's style— "Just as your father always said, you are your own fashion statement."

Considering she still thought Liz was marrying into a family of part-time nudists, Auntie was probably pleased Liz was wearing anything at all.

Smiling to herself, Liz playfully kicked one foot toward the mirror, enjoying how the light shimmered on her silver-threaded stockings. They sparkled over a few inches of leg before disappearing into a pair of thigh-high white boots.

"Cool," said Liz, approving her look. Maybe this was a fake wedding, but it was still her wedding and she wanted to look hot. She tucked back a stray red hair that had tumbled loose from her French roll. George, her neighbor, had helped decorate her wedding-do with sprigs of baby's breath that curled through her hair. Together they had carefully anchored the sprigs—she wanted the small white flowers to survive the Harley ride to Vegas.

Pulling a white silk scarf off her dresser table, she heard the front door of her apartment open.

"Lizzy?"

"Back here, Raven." She carefully wound the scarf around her hair.

"Tuned up your bike, I see."

"Check out the polished
duce carbon buildup." She ha
side when she stayed up late to
easier to lay out some burlap on
into her apartment, where she h
wanted.

Heavy footsteps. Raven stood in h

She gave him an appreciative one
mighty fine, Raven."

He wore a three-piece white suit with
his lapel. His thick black hair was slicked back in a neat
ponytail. And the skull-and-crossbones earring had been
removed, replaced with a simple diamond stud.

"And you look beautiful, Lizzy."

The earnestness in his voice touched her. Sometimes she
thought she was the only one who understood his sweet
nature. Russell had scoffed when she'd said Raven was a
pussycat, but it was true.

Russell.

It hurt to even think his name.

"Raven," she said quickly, forcing herself to think, say,
do anything but dwell on Russell. "Can you knot this scarf
in the back?" She turned around and held the ends of the
scarf at the nape of her neck.

"Sure, Lizzy."

When he took the ends, she jumped. "Your hands are
freezing!"

"Sorry—can't tie a knot." She heard him briskly rub
them together. "Guess I'm, uh…"

The pause was so long that she turned around to make
sure he hadn't gotten lost in one of his time warps.

What she saw surprised and worried her. His chin was
quivering and his eyes were red rimmed. She gathered him
into her arms. As much of him as fitted, anyway.

"Raven, what's the matter?"

"I think my heart needs a tune-up." He sniffed loudly.

She patted his elbow. It was all she could reach. "There,
there. You've been reading too many of those magazines."

...fed again. "Or maybe it's somethin'

...ed the sweet scent of the rose, debating how to ...her question. "Is it because," she said softly, "I ...'t return your affections?"

Brr-ring. The brash ring of the doorbell interrupted her inquiry.

Liz looked toward the sound. "I wonder who that is?"

Another metallic buzz reverberated through the apartment.

"Persistent, aren't they," she mused, glancing back at Raven. "You be okay if I leave for a second?"

He nodded, extracted a handkerchief from his back pocket and loudly blew his nose.

"Okay, stay here. I'll be right back."

On her way through the living room, she unwound the scarf and draped it over the Harley's handlebars. Opening the door, she half expected to see a delivery person with flowers. Gloxinias maybe. A wedding-day gift from Auntie.

Instead, on her doorstep stood a figure from Liz's recent, harrowing past.

Charlotte.

Not the Aphrodite-Terminator, as Russell had nicknamed her after the Hollywood Boulevard scene. But Charlotte the bride. She stood erect, her slim form encased in a floor-length cream-colored satin gown. Her blond hair, pulled back in an elaborate twist, left her face exposed. Which made it easy to read her obvious pain.

Liz, rarely at a loss for words, couldn't think of a single one. She gave Charlotte another once-over. Her wedding dress was smothered in hundreds—thousands?—of tiny pearls. *If those are real,* Liz thought, *I could ransom Charlotte and forget the trust fund.*

Charlotte's words brought Liz back to reality.

"May I come in?" she asked in a wobbly voice.

Liz blinked into Charlotte's stricken expression and, pulling the door open wider, stepped aside. As Charlotte floated past, Liz felt a rush of pity seeing Ms Bel Air's perfectly tapered chin tremble.

Turning to face the door, Liz mentally assessed the situation. *Save the pity for a nobler cause. She didn't find your apartment on a whim. She's here, in her wedding dress, because something horrible has happened.*

Like what?

Liz stared at the peephole, wishing she could peer into it and see the reason for this unexpected visit. Then it hit her.

She knows about the date. She's here to shoot me before she takes her wedding vows.

Liz shut the door with a sharp click. *I'm overreacting.* The only place Charlotte could have hidden a gun was in that overcoifed bun, and she'd hardly ruin an expensive hairdo to conceal a murder weapon. Besides, nothing happened on that date. Well, nothing except Liz's uncensored fantasies, and Charlotte wouldn't know of those unless she were a psychic.

You're safe. Be cool.

Easing out a slow breath, Liz turned to face Charlotte, who stood primly next to the Harley, looking as though she'd stepped out of one of the bridal magazines that Raven so loved. Her hair, her makeup were movie-star perfect. Liz's gaze slid down Charlotte's lace-and-pearl-covered arms to her manicured fingernails that shimmered with peachy ivory polish. No pearls there, at least.

Charlotte sniffled.

Liz met Charlotte's eyes, which were brimming with tears. A jagged path of mascara trickled down one alabaster cheek.

"I'm not doing very well," Charlotte said in a quavering voice. "Do you have a tissue?"

"No." Liz blinked rapidly. She'd never heard anyone pronounce "tissue" without an "ish" sound. "Will toilet paper do?"

Charlotte raised one plucked eyebrow and seemed to think a moment before nodding her assent.

"Bathroom's to the left." *Raven's to the right. And I'm stuck in the middle of this prewedding soap opera.*

Charlotte glided out of the room. Liz heard the bathroom door shut discreetly.

The doorbell buzzed again.

Liz glanced over her shoulder. *The delivery person better be bringing me something stronger than flowers.* She pivoted and headed back to the door. *A vat of margaritas would be nice. Something to fortify me for this Charlotte Encounter of the Third Kind.*

But when she pulled open the door, her heart tumbled. *Russell.*

He looked devastatingly handsome in a charcoal gray tuxedo that matched his eyes. A thickly knotted black-and-white-striped tie added a distinguished flair. He looked every inch the groom, from his buffed black shoes to his neatly combed and parted hair. The latter made her smile wistfully as she remembered his wild postbikeride hair that first fateful night.

Who would have thought that one random encounter would turn her life upside down. Turn her heart inside out.

"May I come in?" he asked in a low tone.

She couldn't find her voice. So she nodded and stepped back. Maybe he was following Charlotte, hoping to stop her before she committed murder. But he seemed awfully cool. Self-assured. Maybe he, too, knew that bun held nothing lethal…

He walked into the room, never taking his eyes off Liz. He seemed to want to say something, then changed his mind.

Finally he gestured to her outfit. "You look…dazzling."

"Thanks." She closed the door and crossed to the bike. Standing next to the mass of chrome and leather made her feel stronger. She pulled back her shoulders. "Aren't you two supposed to be at the church?"

"Yes. Along with three hundred others, who—" he flipped his wrist and checked the time "—are expected to arrive in a little over an hour."

His cocky attitude irked her. Here she was falling apart, and he was giving her a countdown to his wedding. Ducking her head, she pretended to check something on the bike. "Big wedding," she mumbled. Didn't he realize how painful it was to meet him on his wedding day?

"Yes," he murmured. "But not the wedding I want."

She jerked her head up. Their gazes locked. He didn't sound so cocky now. And he looked...wistful. Or, in her own pain, was she imagining that? She wanted him to say more, to explain what he meant, but the moment of silence stretched into awkwardness.

"Care for a drink?" she finally said.

"Wild Turkey?"

"Only water."

"It'll keep me sober. I'll pass."

Liz played with one of the beaded fringes on her bike. "Funny comment to make on the way to your own wedding."

"Liz, I—" Russell stopped himself from saying what had burdened his heart these past few days. "Did I tell you that you look pretty?" he said instead.

"Actually, you said 'dazzling.'"

His mind warred with his heart. He should end this. Leave. She was on her way to her wedding—on her way to her dreams. But her eyes held him. Within their sparkling green depths, he relived every glorious, heat-filled moment of this past week. His gaze dropped to the Harley, and he remembered the rides they'd shared. How his hands spanned her waist. How her exotic scent exploded in the rush of air. They had raced through a sensory world filled with colors and images—but none of it as intoxicating or vivid as the world the two of them had shared.

"We belong together," he blurted out.

Liz glanced toward the bathroom and back. "I'm a dreamer, remember?" she said quickly under her breath. A sadness flickered across her face.

His voice felt heavy, unreal, as he recited what he'd been

repeating to himself these last few days. "I can't throw away my life for dreams—"

"It's cool. No hard feelings." She fumbled with her hair, but he noticed she also brushed at the corner of her eye. "Let's just say it was fun."

But it was more than fun. It was the most alive, most passionate he'd ever felt. He'd lived years in an ivory tower, afraid to step outside and truly experience living. And Liz had ripped that world wide open.

Liz. *A life without her would be a life half lived.*

A second, more powerful, realization hit him in the gut. Maybe his dad had struggled—been a *dreamer*—but he'd been a happy, fulfilled man. If a successful life meant being loved, his dad had been one of the richest men on Earth.

He took a stop toward her. "Liz—"

"Russell!" exclaimed Charlotte, gliding into the room.

"Char!" said Raven, emerging from the bedroom.

Char? Liz cut him a look. His pupils were enlarged. His body shook.

"Char, ain't you supposed to be at the church?" asked Raven.

Charlotte's pink-frosted lips trembled.

"Ain't you?" he repeated, his voice cracking.

She silently mouthed the words, "Yes, but..."

Like two magnets, Charlotte and Raven suddenly fell together. Russell watched in amazement as they clung to each other in the middle of the living room, sniffling and sobbing.

Liz looked at Russell. "Prewedding jitters?"

Charlotte and Raven began kissing passionately.

"More like animal-magnetism jitters," Russell answered drolly.

After a few moments, Raven and Charlotte broke for air. They stared into each other's eyes for so long that Russell was certain they were communicating telepathically.

"I'll start," Charlotte said matter-of-factly, breaking eye contact. Squaring her shoulders, she turned to Russell. "Darling, I'm so sorry."

"Don't tell me—you got a tattoo, too."

"This is serious." She took Raven's hand and inter-twined her fingers with his. "I followed him here because I needed to see him one more time. To tell him that...I love him."

"I love you, too," said Raven in a gravelly voice. He swiped at the corner of his eye.

Charlotte sighed dramatically. "After that fateful scene on Hollywood Boulevard, Rave and I spent some quality time together and...and it was kismet. Please understand. He and I fit together like pennies in a pod."

"Peas—"

"Please, Russell, let me finish. He's not afraid of my money. I can do things for him you'd never let me do for you. I can buy him clothes. And he can work at home, repairing hogs." She looked into Raven's face and smiled warmly.

"Repairing hogs? Why were you always pushing me to be a literary critic—?"

She shrugged. "That was Daddy's idea. But deep down all I ever wanted was a househusband. A man to protect me, love me twenty-four hours a day." She leaned against Raven and made cooing sounds. He nearly eclipsed her in a gentle, beefy-arm hug. They kissed lightly, then looked longingly into each other's eyes.

"My big bad boy," said Charlotte.

"My cover-girl princess," responded Raven.

"I've never known you like this, Char," said Russell, loosening his tie. "How can I not wish you well? You're the happiest I've ever seen you." He knew he should act hurt. At least pretend to feel rejected. But all he felt was immense relief.

He also realized that during this past week, when he had mentally beaten himself up because he felt such over-whelming desire for Liz, he had never been unfaithful to Charlotte. Instead, he had been unfaithful to himself. *The worst infidelity is to marry for the wrong reasons—and I was willing to marry someone to ensure a conventional life. A half life.*

He glanced at his watch. "Three hundred people will be showing up in an hour to see a wedding. Do we have a plan?"

Charlotte took Raven's hand, pulled him close and whispered something in his ear. He nodded.

"Rave and I have decided," she announced, "to return to the church, make a statement of our love and invite everybody to stay for the reception to celebrate our engagement."

"Best idea since Neiman hooked up with Marcus," Russell said. "Tell Wendel to have some emergency martinis ready for your parents and Agnes. Fred, I have a feeling, will be quite fine."

"What will *you* do, Russell?" Charlotte asked, a sad look settling on her features.

"And you, Lizzy," Raven chimed in. "I don't want you to lose your trust fund." His eyes widened. "Say, maybe you can get your neighbor George to marry you—"

"I'm marrying her," Russell said. He'd spent a lifetime speaking from the head, but those words shot straight from his heart. He didn't need to think twice. He'd never wanted anything more in his entire life. "That is, if she'll have me."

Liz parted her red lips but nothing came out.

"Will you marry me, Elizabeth?" he asked quietly. He stretched out his fingers, silently asking her to take his hand.

Liz's heart plummeted more than a story or two. It would be so easy to say yes. But she couldn't. She'd already experienced the pain of a man—her own father—resigning himself to a life of unfulfilled dreams.

"Thanks, but no thanks," she said, her voice barely audible.

Raven's voice boomed through the room. "But you won't get your trust fund, Lizzy—"

"I'm a survivor. I'll get by." How many times these

past few days had she repeated those same words to herself. A hundred? A thousand?

Russell took a step toward her. "I want to share my life with you," he continued, his tone forceful. "From the moment we met, I knew it was right. I was just too blinded by my past to take a chance. Give me that chance, Liz, please." He opened his hands as though he had nothing to hide. "I love you," he added, lowering his voice.

After a beat she answered softly. "I love you, too. But Russell—"

Before she could finish her sentence, he had crossed the room and gently laid his finger against her lips.

"No more Russell. Call me Max."

He dropped his hand to her chin and gently pulled her toward him. Brushing her cheek with his lips, he murmured, "My dream is to marry you. Let me be a dreamer..."

His fingers slid sensuously to her neck. She caught a look of yearning in his eyes before his lips consumed hers. As they kissed, a liquid weakness stole over her, washing away her lingering doubts. It took all her strength to remain standing as he slowly pulled away. This was the man she'd met that first night. Passionate, exciting, daring. The man she had fallen in love with.

She drew in a quick breath and took his waiting hand. "Yes, Max," she said. "Yes, yes, yes."

A short buzz interrupted her acceptance.

All four of them looked at the door.

"Don't tell me there's someone else who wants to marry somebody in this room," Russell said. "We finally got it all ironed out."

Liz headed to the door. "Probably George, wondering why all these brides and grooms are coming to my apartment..." She grasped the knob and pulled.

There stood Auntie in a lilac-and-pink suit, gripping her signature pink handbag. "Dear heart," she said, waltzing inside.

"Auntie?" said Liz, bewildered. "What about the convention?"

"I'm on my way. But I had to drop by—it's important you receive something today." She beamed at Russell, then halted upon seeing Raven and Charlotte. "Oh, my. Your brother is getting married today, too?"

"Just practicin'," Raven said, giving Charlotte a squeeze.

Auntie nodded, then shot a loving look to Liz. "Your wedding gift." She pulled a silver picture frame out of her purse and handed it to Liz. "Because it sealed your fate, it should be given to you the day you take your vows."

Liz swallowed hard as she stared at the picture of her and Russell. Who knew—maybe Auntie's superstitions were true. In this case, it certainly was. The picture had sealed their fate as lovers. "We'll treasure it always, Auntie." She reached over and pressed a kiss on her cheek.

Auntie turned moist eyes to Russell. "Take good care of my beloved niece."

"I will."

Auntie embraced Liz one more time. "Your father would be so proud." She turned back to the room. "All you brides and grooms," she said, her voice filled with awe. "This must be significant. I'll have to think about that." She smiled benevolently at Raven. "Goodbye, Rover. Your fiancée is very pretty. If I had known, I would have taken your picture as well." After blowing a kiss to Russell and Liz, she stepped jauntily out of the apartment and into the sunshine.

When the click-click-click of her heels faded, Russell spoke. "Let's get this hog on the road," he said, waving Liz toward the bike. "We want to get to Vegas before sunset." He nodded to Raven. "Tell Drake we need a best man. Tell him to look for the chapel with Barbie's Harley parked in front—he'll know what that means."

"Mind if we stay and...freshen up before we leave?" Charlotte asked.

"No problem," Liz said, lifting the scarf off the handlebars and wrapping it around her head. After straddling the driver's seat, she turned the ignition. It purred, matching her feelings exactly. "Raven," she called out, "if you need a best man—I mean, woman—I'm your girl."

She felt Russell settle in behind her. As they eased out the front door and bounced down the single porch step, Liz heard Raven yell "Good luck" before slamming the door shut behind them.

Russell squeezed her waist and leaned forward. Pressing his warm cheek against hers, he said, "Watch the speed limit, okay?"

She turned her head, her lips almost touching his. "What's the matter—can't handle fast and wild?"

"Oh, Liz, I wouldn't marry you if I couldn't."

Reach new heights of passion and
adventure this August in

ROCKY MOUNTAIN MEN

Don't miss this exciting new collection featuring
three stories of Rocky Mountain men and the
women who dared to tame them.

CODE OF SILENCE
by Linda Randall Wisdom

SILVER LADY
by Lynn Erickson

TOUCH THE SKY
by Debbi Bedford

Available this August wherever
Harlequin and Silhouette books are sold.

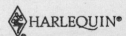 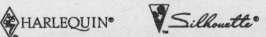

MILLION DOLLAR SWEEPSTAKES
OFFICIAL RULES
NO PURCHASE NECESSARY TO ENTER

1. To enter, follow the directions published. Method of entry may vary. For eligibility, entries must be received no later than March 31, 1998. No liability is assumed for printing errors, lost, late, non-delivered or misdirected entries.

   To determine winners, the sweepstakes numbers assigned to submitted entries will be compared against a list of randomly, preselected prize winning numbers. In the event all prizes are not claimed via the return of prize winning numbers, random drawings will be held from among all other entries received to award unclaimed prizes.

2. Prize winners will be determined no later than June 30, 1998. Selection of winning numbers and random drawings are under the supervision of D. L. Blair, Inc., an independent judging organization whose decisions are final. Limit: one prize to a family or organization. No substitution will be made for any prize, except as offered. Taxes and duties on all prizes are the sole responsibility of winners. Winners will be notified by mail. Odds of winning are determined by the number of eligible entries distributed and received.

3. Sweepstakes open to residents of the U.S. (except Puerto Rico), Canada and Europe who are 18 years of age or older, except employees and immediate family members of Torstar Corp., D. L. Blair, Inc., their affiliates, subsidiaries, and all other agencies, entities, and persons connected with the use, marketing or conduct of this sweepstakes. All applicable laws and regulations apply. Sweepstakes offer void wherever prohibited by law. Any litigation within the province of Quebec respecting the conduct and awarding of a prize in this sweepstakes must be submitted to the Régie des alcools, des courses et des jeux. In order to win a prize, residents of Canada will be required to correctly answer a time-limited arithmetical skill-testing question to be administered by mail.

4. Winners of major prizes (Grand through Fourth) will be obligated to sign and return an Affidavit of Eligibility and Release of Liability within 30 days of notification. In the event of non-compliance within this time period or if a prize is returned as undeliverable, D. L. Blair, Inc. may at its sole discretion, award that prize to an alternate winner. By acceptance of their prize, winners consent to use of their names, photographs or other likeness for purposes of advertising, trade and promotion on behalf of Torstar Corp., its affiliates and subsidiaries, without further compensation unless prohibited by law. Torstar Corp. and D. L. Blair, Inc., their affiliates and subsidiaries are not responsible for errors in printing of sweepstakes and prize winning numbers. In the event a duplication of a prize winning number occurs, a random drawing will be held from among all entries received with that prize winning number to award that prize.

5. This sweepstakes is presented by Torstar Corp., its subsidiaries and affiliates in conjunction with book, merchandise and/or product offerings. The number of prizes to be awarded and their value are as follows: Grand Prize — $1,000,000 (payable at $33,333.33 a year for 30 years); First Prize — $50,000; Second Prize — $10,000; Third Prize — $5,000; 3 Fourth Prizes — $1,000 each; 10 Fifth Prizes — $250 each; 1,000 Sixth Prizes — $10 each. Values of all prizes are in U.S. currency. Prizes in each level will be presented in different creative executions, including various currencies, vehicles, merchandise and travel. Any presentation of a prize level in a currency other than U.S. currency represents an approximate equivalent to the U.S. currency prize for that level, at that time. Prize winners will have the opportunity of selecting any prize offered for that level; however, the actual non U.S. currency equivalent prize if offered and selected, shall be awarded at the exchange rate existing at 3:00 P.M. New York time on March 31, 1998. A travel prize option, if offered and selected by winner, must be completed within 12 months of selection and is subject to: traveling companion(s) completing and returning of a Release of Liability prior to travel; and hotel and flight accommodations availability. For a current list of all prize options offered within prize levels, send a self-addressed, stamped envelope (WA residents need not affix postage) to: MILLION DOLLAR SWEEPSTAKES Prize Options, P.O. Box 4456, Blair, NE 68009-4456, USA.

6. For a list of prize winners (available after July 31, 1998) send a separate, stamped, self-addressed envelope to: MILLION DOLLAR SWEEPSTAKES Winners, P.O. Box 4459, Blair, NE 68009-4459, USA.

As Seen on TV!

Free Gift Offer

With a Free Gift proof-of-purchase
from any Harlequin® book, you can receive
a beautiful cubic zirconia pendant.

This stunning marquise-shaped stone is a genuine cubic
zirconia—accented by an 18" gold tone necklace.
(Approximate retail value $19.95)

Send for yours today...
compliments of ✦HARLEQUIN®

To receive your free gift, a cubic zirconia pendant, send us one original proof-of-purchase, photocopies not accepted, from the back of any Harlequin Romance®, Harlequin Presents®, Harlequin Temptation®, Harlequin Superromance®, Harlequin Intrigue®, Harlequin American Romance®, or Harlequin Historicals® title available at your favorite retail outlet, together with the Free Gift Certificate, plus a check or money order for $1.65 U.S./$2.15 CAN. (do not send cash) to cover postage and handling, payable to Harlequin Free Gift Offer. We will send you the specified gift. Allow 6 to 8 weeks for delivery. Offer good until December 31, 1997, or while quantities last. Offer valid in the U.S. and Canada only.

Free Gift Certificate

Name: _____

Address: _____

City: _____ State/Province: _____ Zip/Postal Code: _____

Mail this certificate, one proof-of-purchase and a check or money order for postage and handling to: HARLEQUIN FREE GIFT OFFER 1997. In the U.S.: 3010 Walden Avenue, P.O. Box 9071, Buffalo NY 14269-9057. In Canada: P.O. Box 604, Fort Erie, Ontario L2Z 5X3.

FREE GIFT OFFER   084-KEZ

ONE PROOF-OF-PURCHASE
To collect your fabulous FREE GIFT, a cubic zirconia pendant, you must include this original proof-of-purchase for each gift with the properly completed Free Gift Certificate.

LOVE & LAUGHTER LET'S CELEBRATE SWEEPSTAKES
OFFICIAL RULES—NO PURCHASE NECESSARY

To enter, complete an Official Entry Form or 3" x 5" card by hand printing the words "Love & Laughter Let's Celebrate Sweepstakes," your name and address thereon and mailing it to: in the U.S., Love & Laughter Let's Celebrate Sweepstakes, P.O. Box 9076, Buffalo, NY 14269-9076, or in Canada to, Love & Laughter Let's Celebrate Sweepstakes, P.O. Box 637, Fort Erie, Ontario L2A 5X3. Limit: one entry per envelope, one prize to an individual, family or organization. Entries must be sent via first-class mail and be received no later than 11/30/97. No liability is assumed for lost, late, misdirected or nondelivered mail.

Three (3) winners will be selected in a random drawing (to be conducted no later than 12/31/97) from among all eligible entries received by D. L. Blair, Inc., an independent judging organization whose decisions are final, to each receive a collection of 15 Love & Laughter Romantic Comedy videos (approximate retail value: $250 U.S. per collection).

Sweepstakes offer is open only to residents of the U.S. (except Puerto Rico) and Canada who are 18 years of age or older, except employees and immediate family members of Harlequin Enterprises, Ltd., their affiliates, subsidiaries, and all other agencies, entities and persons connected with the use, marketing or conduct of this sweepstakes. All applicable laws and regulations apply. Offer void wherever prohibited by law. Taxes and/or duties on prizes are the sole responsibility of the winners. Any litigation within the province of Quebec respecting the conduct and awarding of prize may be submitted to the Régie des alcools, des courses et des jeux. All prizes will be awarded; winners will be notified by mail. No substitution for prizes is permitted. Odds of winning are dependent upon the number of eligible entries received.

Any prize or prize notification returned as undeliverable may result in the awarding of that prize to an alternative winner. By acceptance of their prize, winners consent to use of their names, photographs or likenesses for purposes of advertising, trade and promotion on behalf of Harlequin Enterprises, Ltd., without further compensation unless prohibited by law. In order to win a prize, residents of Canada will be required to correctly answer a time-limited, arithmetical skill-testing question administered by mail.

For a list of winners (available after December 31, 1997), send a separate stamped, self-addressed envelope to: Love & Laughter Let's Celebrate Sweepstakes Winner, P.O. Box 4200, Blair, NE 68009-4200, U.S.A.

LLRULES

Celebrate with

LOVE & LAUGHTER™

Love to watch movies?

Enter now to win a FREE 15-copy video collection of romantic comedies in Love & Laughter's Let's Celebrate Sweepstakes.

WIN A ROMANTIC COMEDY
VIDEO COLLECTION!

To enter the Love & Laughter Let's Celebrate Sweepstakes, complete an Official Entry Form or hand print on a 3" x 5" card the words "Love & Laughter Let's Celebrate Sweepstakes," your name and address and mail to: "Love & Laughter Let's Celebrate Sweepstakes," in the U.S., 3010 Walden Avenue, P.O. Box 9076, Buffalo, N.Y. 14269-9076; in Canada, P.O. Box 637, Fort Erie, Ontario L2A 5X3. Limit: one entry per envelope, one prize to an individual family or organization. Entries must be sent via first-class mail and be received no later than November 30, 1997. See back page ad for complete sweepstakes rules.

Celebrate with Love & Laughter™!

Official Entry Form

"Please enter me in the Love & Laughter Let's Celebrate Sweepstakes"

Name: _____

Address: _____

City: _____

State/Prov.: _____ Zip/Postal Code: _____

LLENTRY

LLENTRY